brief grislys

A Collection of Horror Stories
of 1000 Words or Less

SELECTED & EDITED
BY JOHN R. MABRY

the apocryphile press
BERKELEY, CA
www.apocryphile.org

apocryphile press
BERKELEY, CA

Apocryphile Press
1700 Shattuck Ave #81
Berkeley, CA 94709
www.apocryphile.org

Printed in the United States of America
ISBN 978-1-937002-87-9 paperback
ISBN 978-1-937002-88-6 kindle
ISBN 978-1-937002-89-3 epub

Cover graphics by B.J. West
Editorial Assistance by Kate Gladstone

contents

introduction

By John R. Mabry

The idea was simple: tell the scariest story you can, in less than 1,000 words.

It sounds easy, but it isn't. A lot of the tools on which a horror writer depends are simply not available in such an abbreviated form. For instance, it takes time (and this means word count) to lull your readers into a false sense of security. It takes paragraphs to establish a character that readers will give two figs about—let alone be upset if he or she is in danger. And, of course, the scariest villain or ogre is one that is comprehensible—that evil might have been mine had I been born in a certain situation or been faced with similar choices. *Nisi Dei gratia, eam.* But this, too, takes words to establish.

And when you only have a thousand of them…well, that's a challenge, isn't it? A thousand words sounds like a lot until you start writing. And when you bump up against that limit far short of the end of your tale, what to do? Usually, you must start again, with a merciless eye towards economy.

I solicited these stories from a wide variety of places— Facebook, writer's websites, ads in writers' magazines, etc. The response was enthusiastic—but the stories were of wildly mixed quality, as you might expect. In the end, I rejected more stories than I accepted.

The stories you find here are stories that moved me—scared, intrigued, or amused me. Their selection is entirely subjective—the prerogative of an anthology editor. But I proceeded on the assumption that if a story didn't prick my imagination, make me laugh, or raise my hackles, it probably wouldn't do those things for you, either.

My thanks to all the writers who contributed—especially to those who kept sending stories until our limit of three per author was reached. My special thanks to my editorial assistant Kate Gladstone, and cover artist B.J. West for the great grizzly bear drawing—exactly what I was hoping for.

I hope you enjoy reading these as much as I have. There's nothing like a good jolt of adrenaline, and when such jolts come fast...well, so much the better.

John R. Mabry
Oakland, CA
4/6/13

are you still there?

By Cornelius Fortune

Okay, so I lied to you, it's not that big a deal. You would have figured it out anyway.

There were so many times I wanted to tell you, but we were so much in the moment, I couldn't bear spoiling it—I needed more time. I needed more *you*. What else could I have done? I stalled till the truth came bashing at your door. That word—bashing—I mean, it's really appropriate right about now. You're emotionally bashing me in.

Hey, are you still there?

I don't know when it started. Your sister always knew because I could tell her things that you never would have listened to. We share a dark soul of sorts. We shared lots when you weren't around.

Wait. Don't hang up on me. It wasn't like that. When things went and got hot and heavy, I shut 'em off real quick, but try as I might, the truth about me has a way of leaving people dead....I mean *cold*. She told you things to stir the corn and grind the meal.

I'm afraid for you. You don't understand. I'm *very* afraid for you. Could you just listen, please? I'll let you respond in a minute. You need to take all of this in. It's a glass of water versus consuming an ocean. Here's the Biblical flood, my dear, all of it....

They're going to say I murdered women I found on the Internet—that couldn't be further from the truth. I never murdered women.

I hit my ex-wife over the head with a lava lamp. I didn't think it would kill her, I just wanted to shut her up; she kept saying the same thing, over, and over, and over. She was still alive after it happened (accusing eyes wide with terror)—you have to believe me. It was Bobby Bradley that did something horrible to her body. They never found it, but the whole town thought I did it. I'm not as smart as Bobby Bradley—I would have gotten caught for sure.

Bobby Bradley? Oh, sorry. Sometimes I forget that everybody doesn't know Bobby Bradley, but they would if they followed the RSS feeds, bizarre news, crime reports, Satanic rituals gone way past south, and down to the earth's core. Hell, as much as I talk, I thought everyone was familiar.

Bobby Bradley was my imaginary friend as a kid. As funny as it sounds, we grew up together; hit puberty right about the same time, and then he got that taste for blood and couldn't shake it off; wanted real bad, to be bad. Once, he pushed my mother down the stairs because she wouldn't let us play outside, and *I* got in trouble for it. Can you believe that? I tell him not to do it, but he still goes and does it anyway. He's a cagey bastard.

Are you still there?

Good. I thought I lost you.

Everywhere I go, he finds me. He makes friends with my friends, and he destroys anything I've ever cared about. I have to lie about the person I am. I have to become someone else to protect everybody else. Does that make sense?

So what, my name isn't "Joe-Whatever-You-Thought-It-Was," that's no reason not to love me back, since I loved you when you were just another dirty spam, a webcam exclusive delivered straight to my in-box. Remember you sent that e-mail, "Want to see pictures of me?" And like an idiot, I clicked it, and fell in love, I'm not ashamed to tell you, for the first time ever—again.

We met up at that local bookstore: me with my Nietzsche book, and you with your Stephen King one. Remember? That's how we identified ourselves, by the books we read. You told me your name was Christine, but it wasn't, you just wanted to make sure I wasn't crazy or whatever, which I'm here to tell you, I'm not.

I'm sorry. What was that?

We're breaking up?

Now, wait a sec—oh, you mean *I'm* breaking up. Just give me a minute or two. I'm passing under this bridge, signal's all gone to hell. I guess I need a new phone.

Listen.

I have to save you from him. He's coming. Lock the door. I can protect you from him if you'll just give me the chance.

Don't tell me you believe what they told you? You can't be serious. They're liars!

I didn't mean to raise my voice at you, forgive me.

I'm not mad. I was mad. But I'm not mad anymore. Not at you. Not anymore. I want to take you in my arms and crush you, squeeze the breath out of you. I want to see your eyes pop out of your head. It can be so easy if you let it be.

Oh. *That Sound.*

Car door. I'm parked outside your apartment. See me?

I can see you.

I know. It's a new car. I traded the old one in, got a new license plate, too. The bodies Bobby Bradley had in the trunk were starting to stink up the whole car. It was coming from the vents. Hot days were the worst. There's liquid junk crusted under my fingernails that just won't wash away. I nibble at them absentmindedly, relishing that coppery taste. It's like a prelude to dessert; bits of people under your nails, riding the tip of your tongue, till the slow dissolve takes them away. Old movies used plenty of dissolves for, like, location shifts, dramatic effect. If this were a film, we'd be dissolving to the hero's footsteps, his blade poised and ready—ready to *cut* to the next scene. Ready to triumph over pure evil. Tell me you wouldn't want to see that.

Unlock your door. I'm going to protect you, whether you want it or not.

Cross my heart.

Hope to die.

Stick a needle in your eye.

Are you still there? Hello? Hello?

Hello?

arise

By Derrick Juengst

The black was total. The black was thick. Darkness of night shies away from places like this, a void, nothing. A single drop of water fell though the blackness. It crashed with a splash onto a forehead. At least there was a sound in the nothingness. A gooey eyelid flapped open. If you could see the eye, it would be white on white. Some electrical impulses began to explode inside the body containing the eye. A long dormant fatty matter inside its head awoke to the black. No memories, no desires filled its brain, except one...hunger. Still, the fatty matter inside its head began to take in sensory information on the other parts of its body. Two arms, two legs, it was a start. It began to feel the soft satin pillow its head was resting on. It didn't care. Images in the black flashed onto its one open eye. "A memory?" one might ask. What does that softened eye see in total blackness? Truly, there was only one thing in the fatty matter's mind. Movement: the tattered silk moved around its arms and legs. The rustling noise echoed in emptiness. It understood. It pushed its arms up through the blackness and hit cold heavy stone. The blackness pushed back at the one opened eye. It opened the other one in response, but the same void enveloped all. Still hunger. It realized it had hands at that moment and searched the edges of the void. Not much room. It pushed at the cold stone roof as hard as it could. If it was breathing, it might grunt. It wasn't breathing. A single star flashed through a crack in the side of the roofed enclosure before the arms gave way to utter blackness again. The white on white eyes registered this to a new found connection into the fatty matter. Plans were not to be made: only hunger ruled. Arms pushed again at the stone, this time closer to the lost light. When the light from the star made an appearance, a gray hand shot towards it. A gold cufflink sparkled in the night. The stone roof slammed down on the gray hand, but pain was not something the fatty matter had a comprehension of. Gray fingers peeled around the cement ceiling and lifted and heaved. Stars filled the empty void. The damp air of night welcomed. Black silk fell loosely on bony limbs. Thick black hair sparsely clutched a fleshy skull. Stiff black shoes touched the dewy grass of a not-yet-light morning.

be grateful

By Gianni Washington

When I was five years old, my father pried my fingernails from my fingers, boiled them and ate them. My mother divorced him for being a weirdo, but left me with him because "a growing girl needs her father." And I did need him. I loved my dad. He always pushed my glass closer to my right hand at mealtimes so I could grab it and drink from it once all the fingers on my left hand were gone ("You've got five others, Becky, and besides, I need the nourishment."). He even made me a super-long crazy-straw (that's what he does for a living—makes crazy-straws) that reached all the way across the kitchen when both of my forearms were gone. It was pink and had bits of glitter in it and it curved to make the letters of my name, with a heart in place of the "e" ("Dad, it kind of looks like 'Bocky.'" "Don't you appreciate anything I do for you? *Jesus*, Bocky..." "Dad, my name's Becky." "You see? That is EXACTLY what I'm talking about."). He's a wonderful person, and probably the greatest dad there ever was ("Hey, Frank, what do you have for lunch?" "A turkey sandwich with lettuce and tomato, a strawberry Capri Sun, carrot sticks and some watermelon. What'd you get, Becky?" "A block of sharp cheddar and a pack of Ho Hos." "You got Ho Hos? Dude, your dad is the best!" "I know, right?"). We do everything together. After my eyes were gone, he would take me to the movies and whisper-tell me what was happening in each scene ("Now they're kissing. Still kissing. Now he's taking off her shirt." "OK, Dad." "She's unbuttoning *his* shirt now." "OK, Dad, really—that's enough." "This is great stuff, Becky. You're really missing out."). I don't know what I would have done without him. As you can probably imagine, getting a date was difficult because, you know, people can be really shallow. But my dad was there for me every step of the way. When I turned twenty-three, he started wheeling me to the park in a wagon every day so I could meet people. He would put me on a park bench and go hide behind a tree, because what guy wants to meet a girl *and* her father all at once ("Hey." "Hi! My name's Becky. What's yours?" "Chad." "You have a nice voice, Chad." "Thanks. Your...um...leg looks really great in that skirt." "Thank you. So, do you live around here?" "Yeah." "Where?" "Here." "Here as in...?" "This bench." "Oh. I'm sorry." "Don't be. I haven't had company in quite a while." "Really? I thought this park was pretty popular." "Nah. Not since the stabbings." "The what?" "Stabbings. People don't really come here anymore. Scared to, but I think it's kind of exciting. A few of them happened right where you're sitting." "I see...")? All in all, I've had a good life. Some people starve, get into freak accidents, lose everything they have. But I have a roof over my head, air in my lung, and a terrific dad who loves me. What more could a girl ask for?

a better tomorrow

By Morgen Knight

Devon Gary looked into the eyes of the woman who had bumped into him, and felt a deeply familiar stirring. She was in her sixties (at least), with white hair framing her black, lined face. She'd said "Excuse me," but her eyes had lingered on his once they'd met. "No problem," he'd said. She'd smiled sweetly, painfully, then continued down the hospital corridor.

He couldn't help but wonder at whatever had reacted within himself. He was sure that he'd never met her before.

Thoughts about the mysterious woman occupied his mind as he walked around the hospital, ultimately finding himself back in the maternity ward. He'd been here the better part of three days, leaving only at night. His wife, Shawntee, had come in on Wednesday, believing the baby was coming. False alarm, but the doctors had seen something in their tests and had asked her to stay for observation. Earlier today, Shawntee *had* started contractions, so the baby *was* on the way. But it was taking its time—ten hours so far—and he'd needed a breather. This was his second child; Markus, their first, had been much easier on his wife. Devon stood at the observation window overlooking the cribs of the new arrivals. He'd looked down at Markus from this exact spot.

"Beautiful, huh?" the man said.

Devon hadn't noticed him. "Yeah." The man was older—a grandfather, most likely. He inexplicably reminded Devon of his father. Hauntingly so.

"Something about looking at new life helps clear the mind."

Devon nodded. That was exactly it. "All the potential." The man's brown eyes met his, and he felt the same familiarity wash over him as with the woman.

"Shawntee will be fine," the man said. "Strong woman."

Devon was taken aback. "You know her? Do...I know you?"

The man smiled. "We don't have much time."

"Sir—"

"Markus is a smart boy. Smarter than you know. He'll be at MIT at seventeen, on scholarship."

"Markus, my son?" He was three. "Do I know—"

"But the world is about to change. And you got to make a hard decision right now. The future is bloody and painful. Ain't freedom but death. It's already startin', but you can't see it yet. Not for twenty years more. And then it's too late." He bored his eyes into Devon. "I ain't supposed to be here. But our boy is a smart one and he knew this was the only chance. He got us into the facility, and I hate to think what it cost him." He blinked. "But it don't matter, if you listen." He grabbed the outer arms of Devon. "Forget the cost. This is about the world. A future."

"Sir—" He tried to pull away, but the man held him fiercely.

"The boy in that center crib, he's a monster. You don't understand. But it don't have to be. You can stop it."

"Are you okay?"

"So many don't need to die. There was a chance to change it before he came along. But after...you got to do it." He stopped as if listening. He began to cry. "I'd tell you every secret you have if I could. To make you believe. There ain't much time. I'd do it, but Nature won't allow the paradox. That's what Markus explained. But you're here, this is your time. Give our sons a chance." He fixed him with a hard look, willing him to understand.

"I really think a doctor should hear—"

"Never mind," he said, dejected. "We didn't think you'd listen. Shawntee is the open one. I've always been too hard-headed." He turned away, slumped, and started down the corridor. His body broke up into wavy, crystalline portions. Light shone through him, and then he seemed to walk into thin air, vanishing.

Devon was shocked. His mind tried to wrap around it all. He heard the commotion but it didn't register. And then he turned. A cry escaped him. Shawntee, in her green hospital gown, was in the nursery. She was crying, one hand cradling her belly, the other holding a scalpel. Light glinted off the blade. Already the encounter with the man was fading, dreamlike. Devon pounded on the glass. "Shawntee! Shawntee!"

She looked up and mouthed she was sorry.

"What are you doing!?" His words fogged the glass.

She was weeping, disoriented. "Which one! Which one did I say? Did you see me, old and afraid?" she asked. "Which one?"

"What are you doing? Stop! Shawntee, please stop."

She didn't. Weeping, near the center, she moved crib to crib, stabbing the children. One and then another. Their blood and cries were so red. Alarms were sounded, nurses and doctors screamed. She looked at Devon only once. "It's for our sons," she said, moving—as nurses yanked on the locked nursery door—to the next screaming child.

buried soldiers

By Keith Deininger

Moist earth, mold, fungus ripped from the ground and flung about; the full moon like a sweating fruit; the night breeze like malaria breath; it was intoxicating; it made his head spin with delight. He could feel his brother's Dexedrine churning through him, making his face hot; licking and chewing his lips raw; smelling his own hot breath like craw-dad guts in too much heat. They were here—somewhere—buried in the loamy topsoil.

He'd been a kid, many years ago, playing alone in the tall grass; in a fever; home sick from school, his vomit still steaming in a corner of the back yard. Second Division Bravo Company had been on a search and destroy mission, all jazzed up, hunting cautiously through the grassy jungle. Charlie had an ambush set up on the next hill, lying motionless in the mud like an alligator waiting for the petting zoo to open. He could remember getting mud on Bravo Company as he moved their green plastic bodies up the center of the garden; the mud had been slick and unpleasant, his stomach boiling. He'd run to the corner of the yard to further add to his previous swirl of vomit. Unfortunately, his mother had seen and ushered him back indoors. The next day he'd searched fruitlessly; he'd not found his buried soldiers.

He'd always known, however, even years later, he could find them when he really wanted to. He'd moved away, grown up, stopped talking to his parents. He visited the backyard from time to time, even though there was some young couple living there now, taking to the garden on his own search and destroy missions. He wasn't well liked by the young couple; they threatened to call the police. The young man chased him away with a kitchen knife while his wife watched from the porch, her hands rubbing absently at her swelling belly. Another time he'd heard an earth-shattering crunch behind him and looked up to see the young man with a hunting rifle, thin curling smoke leaking from its barrel. He started coming only at night, figuring he'd be harder to spot.

Now, he knew he was close. He'd torn through the entire yard, trampling the flowers, hurling the uprooted roses every which way. His stick dredged the soil; his head whirled; he grunted and wheezed, his mouth clammy enough to produce a hard pearl of gunk halfway down his throat. His stick cracked into something; he knew it; he'd finally found them. He brought his stick down again, listening to that satisfying crunch. Oh, to finally feel the weight of those soldiers in his hands, to cleanse the dirt from their rubbery plastic bodies. Something small flew up from the hole he'd been digging; it flashed in the moonlight. He dropped his digging stick and reached for the object, cupping it gingerly. It was a tooth, rectangular and white, a gray fleck of gum-flesh hanging from one side. He threw it away in disgust and peered into the churned soil he'd been rooting in; the upper jut of bone stuck up at him from the soil, lined with gleaming teeth.

God damn it, now he was forgetting where other things were buried. He snatched his digging stick and swung it up above his head; he brought it down, swung it up, brought it down.

careless love

by Edward Lodi

"It is a very popular fancy that when a maiden, who has loved not wisely but too well, dies forsaken and broken-hearted, she comes back to haunt her deceiver in the shape of a white hare. The phantom follows the false one everywhere, mostly invisible to all but him. It sometimes saves him from danger, but invariably the white hare causes the death of the betrayer in the end."

—Robert Hunt, *Popular Romances of the West of England,* 1871

"Drowned herself. Just last week."

"Oh? How very sad. Such a comely wench."

"You knew her?"

Masterson reached for the decanter and poured himself an ample glass. "Slightly."

Williams fiddled with his napkin. "They say she was with child."

Masterson shrugged. "Careless of her." He drained the glass in one fierce draft and promptly poured himself another.

"Jolly good shooting today," his friend said, to change the subject.

"Quite so." Masterson seized the loaf, tore off a crust, and wolfed it down with liberal washes of port. "Cook's damnably slow with dinner."

"Our fault, really," Williams said. "We were late getting back."

"And late in skinning that brace of hares."

Williams nodded in agreement. "That albino gave me quite a start. Popped up from nowhere. I was too quick to pull the trigger. Came close to wounding your favorite hound. Sorry about that."

"No harm done. You did me a favor, killing that hare. Sounds queer, but I could swear it's been haunting me all week. Dogging my footsteps, as if it wanted to be shot, yet vanishing whenever I took aim. Good riddance, I say."

"And good dinner, let us hope," Williams quipped, as the servant brought on a steaming pot.

No sooner had he been served than Masterson lit into his plateful with gusto.

* * *

Williams later described what happened. "Too much appetite, I fear, along with too much drink. Masterson bit off more than he could chew, poor chap. Choked to death on a hare bone, of all things."

the circus man

By Dede Ryan

It was Pete's turn to tell a story around the campfire. No one expected much. He was a quiet boy who rarely said "boo." Over the past few weeks, we'd begun to save his story for last, because we could count on him to wind down the night and peacefully put the other boys to sleep. Then he told us about his dream.

"The dreams started when I was four," he began quietly. "And, to this day, when I'm least expecting it, when I've had a good day and when all is right with the world; when I have nearly forgotten the vivid colors of the striped coat, the smell of the wolf, and the hollow stare of the circus man, then the dream comes back."

Ralph, the other counselor, and I looked from face to face at the twelve boys around the fire. A chill ran through the tall pines and tamaracks that circled us, and the fire momentarily burned sideways as if a giant had exhaled over it in one colossal breath. We drew closer to the glowing logs, pulling our sleeping bags tighter around us.

"The first night the circus man came to my room, I was sure he was real," Pete continued. "It had been an ordinary day, but the night was darker than any I had ever known.

My little sister was asleep in her crib in the same room as me. When the circus man and his wolf showed up, I tried to scream. But my vocal cords wouldn't work. It wasn't that I didn't scream for fear of waking her; I just didn't scream for fear.

"There were only 6 or 8 inches, at most, between my bed and the wall where the circus man stood. He wore white linen pants, a bright blue-and-white-striped suit coat, and a clown-like red bow-tie at the collar of a white shirt. He had a straw hat on his long, thin head and held a cane in one white-gloved hand that rested on top of the covers next to my right leg. He was close enough that I should have felt the warmth of his hand through the light blanket. But I did not. Instead, it felt cold as ice.

"I thought if I stayed really, really still, no harm would come to me. It seemed as if hours passed. Though I felt like my eyes were slammed shut against the intruder, I knew they must have been open, because I kept watching the circus man even as he stared back at me.

"His eyes were a color and intensity like none I've seen before or since. They were deep, dark black in the center, rimmed with yellow-brown, like the color of a drink that my Dad has at night. My Dad says the drink is warm and relaxing. But there was nothing warm or relaxing about those eyes that were fixed on mine, and they gazed out of a sunken face that was as white as death itself. He had weak, gray-white lips that formed neither a smile nor a frown, and he had one reddish-blue canker sore in one corner of his mouth. The circus man didn't blink or move at all. I couldn't really detect any breath or motion of breathing. His gloved hand, holding the cane, continued to rest on my bedcovers and his other hand, his left, fell into the crack between my bed and the wall.

"And as he watched me, without motion or sign of his intentions, my wide-panicked eyes moved from the circus man to the white wolf at his side. The wolf stood sideways, in that small space between my bed and the wall where nothing should have been. He was facing me, also staring, with yellow eyes that in intensity matched the eyes of his master, the circus man. The wolf, too, made no motion towards me and showed no signs of breath. His chest did not rise and fall. His nostrils did not flare. But, like a well-wound metronome, his broad white tail brushed slowly over my bedclothes, first one way, then the other, keeping rhythm to some invisible inner music. There was a musky smell of wild animal about him, an earthy saliva odor that mixed with a vague suggestion of stale popcorn in the room.

"The wolf's tail continued to swish back and forth. The urine-colored eyes met mine, and the circus man looked only at me. I tried again to scream—to summon the safety of my parents, to rouse my sister and hear her reassuring cry. But no words would come. The tail continued to move across my covers. And then, just as the two had appeared out of nowhere, they returned to that same place."

Ralph and I surveyed the damage around the campfire. Eyes were as wide as the eyes of the circus man and his wolf.

"What happened then?" asked Stevie, cautiously filling the silence that followed Pete's story.

"Then?" he asked. "I fell asleep."

"Did you ever see the circus man again?" Stevie wanted to know.

"That's the scary part," answered Pete. "He and his wolf still come to my room, and I never know when it will be. Although after years and years, they have never physically hurt me, it would almost be a relief if they did."

It was time to drown the last crackling of fire and get the boys to bed. We dragged our sleeping bags to the tents and eventually went to sleep. All was quiet until we heard the unmistakable howl of a wolf, and the far-off carnival sound of a calliope.

a cooler passion

By Bryan D. Tolin

From his twenty-first story window, he watched as the air-porter bus pulled up. The lobby would be packed with people checking in—a veritable children's rhyme played out in glorious Technicolor. There were the fat ones, short ones, tall ones, black ones, white ones, Asians, blondes, brunettes, and the rare but preferable red heads. They were preferable perhaps *because* they were so rare—the naturals, at any rate. Personally and privately, he hated crowds, but in his line of work, more often than not, they worked in his favor, as they tended to offer variety, and greater odds for success. Hopeful at the prospect, he decided it was time to gamble, to start the day and press the limits of his fortune. He'd soon see if what happened in Vegas *stayed* in Vegas.

Hours later, he shaved the tensions of the day away. The cool running water flowed into the sink, and with it went the remnants of his five o'clock shadow. Ultimately successful, it had been rough going at first—the search for the ideal location to set up shop. But he was used to the grind: the inevitable, tiresome but necessary "meet and greets" with hotel guests, conventioneers, cheating spouses, and yes, finally, his target audience. It took time, but in the end the payoff for him was always more than acceptable, and the target of his affections usually never had second thoughts. Usually.

Today had been different. Today, deep in the depths of the city of sin, he had managed to find someone with a conscience—someone who, at the very last moment, had developed reservations about seeing it through. In the end, a convincing promise of stealth, and an additional cocktail had been enough for her to throw caution to the wind, and the deal was done. Signed, sealed, and delivered straight to his room for several hours of what he defined as "unbridled passion." Though, historically, the women of his choosing had not been so enthusiastic, or understanding.

Now, as he washed and reflected, he took stock in his satisfaction. This had been a great start, with hopefully more to come. After all, the weekend had just begun, and he was, contrary to what his age might suggest, not quite over the hill just yet. More than capable, he was still virile, agile, and able. In reality, he was just getting started.

His companion of the last few hours was in the shower, as he had been moments before. He could see her warm, delicate, still form through the textured glass. Her red hair sparkling just so as the water washed the last traces of the evidence of his "passion" away. The memory was fresh, and in an effort to finish what he'd begun, he would see her again later in the evening. He stared at the mirror and smiled at the thought.

After a brief nap, he grabbed the green cooler from the closet, and filled it with his usual fare . As predicted, the elevator going down was overcrowded. The doors closed, and the lift began its descent. One of the more lively and intoxicated partygoers took notice of the cooler around the eighteenth floor.

"Looks like you're ready to party!" he said, the stench of scotch lingering with that of light laughter.

"Actually, it's a severed head," the man replied with an ever-so-slight smile. After a few moments, he broke into a laugh which relaxed the remaining occupants of the compartment, who eventually joined in at the joke.

"Damn man, you had me for a second."

"Sorry to disappoint," the man replied, and the laughter grew. Game on. "It's actually an arm," at which point the partier with the breath of scotch positively lost control, and the elevator erupted with a fresh dose of laughter.

The man continued, "She threatened to tell my wife...I said enough was enough...you know how it goes."

"I hear that," came a cry from a sympathetic man in the rear. After a few more anonymous agreements, the elevator came to a rest at the casino floor. The man stepped out to let the crowd disperse, then entered the elevator once more in the next stage of his journey to the garage. In doing so, he wished everyone well, as they did him.

"Good luck," he said to everyone as the door closed, and the ride began. They had all been nice enough. If they'd have asked, it would have been no trouble to show them the truth.

The forecast for that night was looking dim. Rain was expected, possibly thunder, slowing down his work outside the city limits slightly. If he could get back, and clear out the shower before midnight, he'd have more than enough time for another tryst before morning.

Perhaps he'd simply order room service.

custody of the chain

By A. J. Barry

Crickets serenaded Jim as he dragged the two half-filled garbage cans to the end of the driveway. That's how it was done at Grandma's house, cans filled halfway, since she usually had to take out the trash. Yet, while Jim was home from college on spring break, he tried to help out as much as possible.

Walking back to the dilapidated two-story farmhouse, Jim realized how much more work needed to be done. He'd already repaired some siding panels, the leaky roof, and a cracked window pane, but the leaning wooden porch with its peeling paint looked more like kindling than the entrance to a home.

As he reached the porch, chaos erupted from the road, generated by a roaring car's engine and the mad, howling laughter of its driver. A silver sedan skidded to a stop at the end of the driveway, and the driver leapt out to pull something from the backseat. He eyeballed Jim, who stood paralyzed with indecision, and then tossed a heavy trunk next to the garbage cans.

"She's all yours now! She wants you!" the madman screamed before hopping back into his car. Then with the same suddenness that marked his arrival, the car sped off, its tail lights fading from sight down the long country road.

Jim waited to see what came next, but there was nothing. There was only the chirping of crickets, and the hairs on the back of his neck came to rest. He should have turned around and not gotten involved, but who was "*she*" and why was he chosen? If he left the trunk, the garbage men would surely take it, either for benefit or trash. While considering his options, he was unaware that his feet had already carried him down the driveway to the black, antique trunk.

Jim hauled it to the perimeter of the porch lights, just to peek inside. The rusty latch opened easily, and in the dim lights he thought he saw a fur coat inside. As he pulled it out he realized it was in pieces, or more precisely, chunks—and they had features. He was holding the body of a dead black cat. Around its neck was not a collar but instead a long rope, which had obviously been used to hang it. He continued pulling on the rope and discovered another dead cat, and then another—a chain of dead black cats. It was horrible, but he couldn't resist seeing it in its entirety. Jim respectfully lifted the cats out, one at a time, seven in all. At the bottom of the trunk lay a manila envelope with his name, James Turner, written on it in black marker.

"Jimmy? What are you doing out there?" called Grandma from inside.

He snapped to the present and called back, "I'll be right in." He picked up the envelope and quickly stuffed the cats back in the trunk.

"Jimmy, where are you at?" yelled Grandma.

Thinking she might be coming, Jimmy shoved the trunk into a dark space under the porch. "Just a minute!" he yelled back.

Then came a scream, and the sick, unmistakable sound of a body tumbling down the stairs. Knotted worms turned in Jim's stomach as he rushed inside.

Grandma, her neck twisted and bent in a grotesque fashion, was bunched up at the bottom of the staircase. Jim grabbed the kitchen phone and dialed 911.

The medics arrived soon but were only able to offer their condolences. The police arrived later but only offered questions that Jim was hesitant to answer. He explained that he was taking out the garbage, but instinctively withheld the incident with the trunk.

"So you were outside. Then you called her to come downstairs?" asked the officer.

"No, she called to me asking 'Where are you at?' while I was still outside," explained Jim, aggravated and emotional. But this time it didn't sound right when he repeated Grandma's line. Maybe her last words sounded more like, "Where did you get a cat?"

He remained silent about the trunk but as the police car backed out of the driveway, a black cat ran past, appearing and then disappearing through the beams of the headlights. Jim wished he'd never touched that cursed trunk... or that envelope which he later found next to the phone in the kitchen.

You are now in possession of the Cat o' Nine Lives. She has chosen you. If you can catch the cat, your curse will end. Until then, I'm sorry. I can only offer you the hope that I have survived and that you may too.

* * *

She always seemed to be there, prowling in the shadows. Watching.

Jim spotted her as he crawled from the wreckage of his car accident. She was there again, outside the doctor's office, when he was diagnosed with Cotard's Syndrome. And once more when a letter arrived to announce his expulsion from school. Each tragedy was witnessed by that relentless black cat.

Then, while making dinner in the old farmhouse, Jim severely lacerated his thumb. It would need stitches and yet the cat was nowhere to be found. In an act of inspiration, he blended the fresh blood with milk in a saucer and set it just inside the front door.

At half past midnight, the cat slipped into the house, yearning for a taste, and Jim stepped from behind the door, slamming it shut.

It wasn't long before the cat was hanging from an old pine tree. Then, Jim added it to the chain of perfectly preserved black cats, eight in all.

That's when the nightmarish visions began. It was Lucille Yardley of Owensboro, Kentucky. Jim didn't know the older black woman but her screaming voice, her revolting face, tormented him day and night until he embarked on the ten hour road trip.

"Hey boy, whatcha doin'?" Lucille called from her apartment window as he delivered her trunk.

dark fresco for a bistro

By Paul Sohar

Are rats also people? Are people also rats? Questions, recalcitrant questions. Leave the word "rat" blank and substitute whatever other beings come to mind or make headlines in the news, and the result will be the same. The main objective of my experiments with metempsychosis at this initial phase has been the development of methodology rather than the tabulation of the results my studies have afforded so far.

It is much too early to draw conclusions yet; however, I have decided to yield to public pressure and the urgings of my colleagues to speak about my work by simply describing one experiment out of the many that I have already reported in the Annals of Metempsychic Research, where the technical details can be found by those who wish to get more deeply involved.

The Bistro is full. I take the last table squeezed into a solid row of other tables. The jungle is dressing for the night, I observe sitting down. On my right a hungry-green multiply-stranded vine, maybe an escaped liana, is eating her way through the tables: while the devil, disguised as a devilish dashing rhino, is taking chunks of a blond face on my left. A warm wind is poured out from a silver decanter by an unshaven smile in the next row, but I'm not quite ready for it yet. I have to share the table with a rather large dog— an Afghan or a Great Dane, I don't know exactly what— I postpone the question for later even though he's not eating, just sitting there as if waiting for me to put in my order. Waiter, let's have a bottle of Grigio; yes, I know it means gray but really white, but if it's black, so be it. I sip it with the Doberman(?) looking on. I'm waiting for the shameless liana to get to him, but she's busy winding herself around the ears of a fat pig who is chewing his gold teeth and inhaling the night from the table in great globs. My plate comes. How come it's empty? Why, oh yes, it's for the bones…Well then, let's get started. Maybe the tongue first. It's practically hanging in my face, this Dalmatian(?) is licking my chops with it. All I have to do is raise my steak knife, slice it off, and pop it in my mouth. And then a sip of the Grigio. Of course it's black, the whole night is dissolved in it: all its colors, aromas and sounds. But the dog resists giving up its haunch, or else the knife is dull. So I bite right into the jugular, the way I should have started; bad manners, but in this confusion…The German shepherd(?) goes limp and starts barking uncontrollably. Or is it the devil on my left? Could be, because his dark horns have gouged the ceiling, letting cats fly out of the sky. Dessert? No, not really, but maybe later. I'll share it with my canine companion. He must be getting hungry by now. It's only fair that I should catch a flying kitten and let him have it. He gulps it down with great gusto and a grateful smile. I hope he's not going to get sick on me and throw up all over this breath-weight shirt I'm wearing— it would dissolve in the warm tide. The cat's whiskers are still sticking out of his jaws and threatening growls pump his gullet. I pour myself another glass of wine and ask for *l'addition, s'il vous plait*. The liana, obviously still hungry, is curling herself around my chair, nibbling on my breath and then my belly button... There's no hurry, sit down wherever you find an empty table and let it swallow you up, let a new set of teeth reshape your life in the Bistro. Is that right? I look around me, and indeed the customers are disappearing one by one. Yet the tables are there. Well fed and ready to retire. It's time to sleep. My eyesight is beginning to fail me, my ears are stuffed up with the slush of chitchat and accordion strains, I'm being pulled into the darkness of the table, I feel the silverware working over my throat. Another meal is over in the Bistro, another night has captured me. Oh, so what, we all know the jungle may be real but the night is only for show.

The first question most readers will ask is: Who is the speaker? A rat, a human, or a table? And of course that's the wrong question. If tables could only speak! I can already hear the weary sigh of earthly wisdom rising and floating off over the ever-receding horizon.

But tables do speak to those who listen. And that's the purpose of an experiment: to listen. The question is how. By bits and pieces the methods are being worked out and as the above experiment shows, a more coherent picture is beginning to emerge. Rats don't need a spokes-rat, they all know the answer. They have no social problems, no leaders, no heroes, and no revolutions. They are true democrats. They have achieved their Utopia.

dark meat

By Paul Stansbury

"Tastes like chicken."

"Give it a break. I don't see this as a time for humor."

"Ease up on him, Ed, I think he's just commenting on the food."

"Same goes for you too, Jeffrey! Let's just drop it."

"Hey, I mean it," Albert said as he studied the morsel perched on the tip of his fork. "Though I wouldn't say it tastes like the best chicken I ever had. No, not even close. But chicken just the same. You know, the best I ever had was the fried chicken at Willie Mac's. Man, that was some kind of chicken. Me, I liked the dark meat. You know what they say, 'The closer to the bone, the sweeter the meat.'"

"Listen, stupid, nothin' that ever came out of that computerized garbage disposal of a food prep unit ever tasted like chicken or anything else you'd want to eat," Ed grumbled as he stared down at his plate. "No matter how much artificial flavoring it adds and lumpy sauce it dumps on top, and whether it calls it Peking Duck or chicken à la king, it still tastes like hinge grease on rubber bands."

The three sat silently for a few minutes staring down at the meager portions on the plates before them. The harsh glare of the ship's lights made their skin appear wan against the stainless steel of the table top.

Then Jeffrey looked up and said, as if the conversation had never paused, "Alligator."

"What?"

"Alligator. Had it once in Louisiana. That's what this tastes like: alligator."

"Damn, not you too!"

"Don't think I ever tasted alligator," Albert declared. "What's it taste like?"

"Little bit like this," Jeffrey cooed, patiently pointing to his plate, "only much, much better. Had it down in New Orleans one Mardi Gras. Alligator étouffée at Boochie's on the Levee."

"What's an ate too fay?" Albert asked.

"About the best thing you ever put in your mouth. Comes from the French word meaning 'smothered.' The locals say it tastes like dark-eyed women and zydeco."

"I'm warning you, put a cork in it," Ed growled.

The three again sat in awkward silence, avoiding eye contact. The only sound was the drone of the engines which occasionally sent a shudder rolling through the ship.

"Both of you are wrong," Ed stated emphatically.

Albert and Jeffrey looked up at him inquisitively. He was still glaring at the plate that sat on the table in front of him. Then he looked up and gave each a smug glance."It was in Peru."

Albert and Jeffrey exchanged glances as if to ask each other if Ed had finally gone completely mad.

"In Cuzco. That's where I had it. Guinea pig, first cousin to a rat. That's what this stuff tastes like," he said stabbing a finger at his plate. "The most godawful stuff you ever put in your mouth. A stringy, foul mess. It's the damn national food down there; like hamburgers back home. It was like eating chunks of bulkhead gasket. I don't even think they skinned the damn things. Tasted like something ugly and dead and it lingered deep in the back of my throat so even half a dozen Pisco Sours couldn't wash out the taste. Just like this stuff." With that he shoved his plate away and put his head down. "Damn that Jürgen," Ed spewed. "Why did that little bastard have to go and screw everything up?"

"Hey, it wasn't all Jürgen's fault," Jeffrey offered timidly. "He had nothing to do with the dark energy drive failure."

"Listen, stupid number two: if Jürgen hadn't been selling spare parts, among other things, on the black market to pay off his gambling debts, we—the crew of Space Freighter 571—wouldn't be in our little predicament now, would we?"

"He's got a point there," Albert chimed in between chews.

"Exactly, if Jürgen hadn't been up to his little tricks, we might have had some real food and something to fix the damn drives," Ed hissed, slamming his fist to the table, rattling the silverware. "If the little jerk hadn't frozen to death while hiding in the deep freeze, I swear I would have strangled him with my own bare hands."

"Well, at least he saved you the trouble," Jeffrey sniped back, "or were you looking forward to it?"

"No, it wasn't like that. But you'll have to admit that he left us in the lurch."

"And . . . and it's not like he's not helping in his own way, him . . . being gone and all. You know, one . . . less mouth to feed . . . and . . . and . . . " Albert stammered.

"And what?" Ed spumed, throwing his cup across the room.

They fell into a sullen silence. After a while, Albert—mustering his courage— asked, "How long until we make port?"

"I ran the numbers again," Jeffrey said without looking up. "Nothing has changed. Without the dark energy drives, it will take us about 6 weeks."

"How much is left, Ed?"

"How much what?"

"Come on, you know, how much food?"

"Food? Well that's been gone for a week. But if you are referring to Jürgen à la king," Ed snorted, pointing to his plate, "there's about two weeks' worth, if you don't make a pig of yourself."

"Did you put all of him in the food prep unit?"

"Yes," Jeffrey said quietly as he swallowed the last forkful from his plate. With one sweep of his hand, Ed stuffed the rest of his portion into his mouth and started chewing noisily while glaring wide-eyed at his two companions.

"But what do we do when we run out of Jürgen?" Albert asked plaintively.

Ed looked at Albert and Jeffrey with a wry smile on his face, while spittle, dotted with flecks of dark meat, ran down his chin. "Well, that's certainly food for thought. Ain't it, boys?"

deadly

By Leah Hampton

Walter was not afraid of spiders. He had never been afraid of them, even when he was a damn kid. So the fact that there was a grotesquely fat, juicy, eight-legged mother creeping across his left eyeball at the moment did not bother him. Not one bit.

Walter's vision was blurred, maybe from the accident or maybe just because she was right on his eye. He watched as the spider's front pincers moved in and out slowly. He was not afraid. In fact, he told himself, when you put a spider in soft focus and get really close like this, they're kind of beautiful. The pincers squished together again, shiny with spider spit.

In the last few minutes, Walter had gone from cruising in criminal glory under a sapphire sky to lying sideways in a heap, frozen and glaring involuntarily at nothingness. Well, almost nothingness. He didn't know where he had landed, or how far he had been thrown, but he did know that there was a whole lot less going on than there had been a little while ago.

Walter had always heard that people never remember traumatic accidents. One of God's little bonuses to the human race—forgetfulness in the face of extreme suffering.

Well, God apparently hated Walter. He could remember everything from the last hour: the wind in his face as he drove, the weight of seven hundred thousand stolen dollars pressing against his side from inside a stuffed leather portfolio (emblazoned with the logo of his ex-wife's company), the anticipation of total, utter freedom. Then a tiny, black dot of distraction, swatting and swerving to avoid the bug's bite... and lastly, instantaneously, the slipping of a tire, the screaming of metal, the sensation of sailing through shattered glass and crisp April air before landing...wherever.

He thought about moving his foot, but it didn't respond to his half-hearted command. As if to mock his immobility, the spider raised a womanly leg with slow, sexy carelessness and brushed her glittering eyes. She seemed to be primping herself for something, and Walter worried that she might be preparing to eat a tasty eyeball salad.

In the periphery of his single eye's view, Walter noticed a fluttering, feather-like object coming in to frame. Between the spider's legs, he saw one, then five, then hundreds of them, arcing and diving intermittently. *The cash*, he thought. *The goddamn cash.*

So much for his plans. His body was shot; there was no way he could move, let alone pick up the money. Eventually, someone would come along and help themselves to his hard-earned embezzlement. The crazy thing was, Walter didn't care. He didn't feel remorse; he didn't feel oh-god-please-help-me-I'm-sorry-I'm-such-a-bastard-I'll-never-do-it-again. He didn't even care if he wound up in prison. *Do they have special prisons for paraplegics?* He figured whoever came along would take his money, but maybe, just maybe, they would also take him to the goddamn hospital.

The spider suddenly reared and scampered off his eye, clearing his vision at last. Walter thought he could almost feel his little eight-legged girlfriend hiding in the collar of his shirt. The money seemed to have settled around him, so he could once again see the beautiful sky that had preoccupied him before.

"Holy crap, are you dead?" Walter realized his ears were working. *Who's there?* "Dude, this is messed up. Holy shit." The same voice again, only closer this time. "Hey, can you hear me? Yo, man." Walter fumed. The person who had come to his rescue was obviously the stupidest organism on the face of the earth. *Yes, dumbass. I am messed up and I can hear you. Now would you mind doing something about it?*

"He-ey.... Where'd all this money come from? Oh, duu-ude!"

Nice. Good for you, crackhead. Now fill your pockets and call nine-one-fucking-one.

A series of rustlings, "hell, yeah"s, and scampering followed. Dumbass was scrambling to pick up as much cash as he could while Walter lay there, wondering if his knight in shining imbecility would think to check if he was still breathing.

Eventually, a fuzzy-headed hippie wearing an outrageously tacky Hawaiian shirt knelt over Walter's open eye.

"Hey, man. Thanks for bringin' the green!" Dumbass leaned down and scrunched up his sunburned forehead. "Hello? Hey, can you blink or anything?"

Somehow, miraculously or perhaps accidentally, Walter did just that. He blinked.

"Heavy, dude. You're, like, seriously damaged here." Dumbass' face suddenly looked a little more human. A little smarter even.

"Yeah, man. I'm gonna get back in my truck and call my cousin, OK? We'll get you some help." *Yeah, man. You do that. I'll just stay here, if that's OK.*

Just as Dumbass began to stand up, Walter felt a sensation on his neck. Spider girl was awake. Suddenly, the little black beauty streamed across his line of sight, straight up at Dumbass' filthy neck.

"Ow!" cried Dumbass, slapping his skin. "Damn. Somethin' bit me. Mother of—"

Walter watched horrified as Spider jumped again, this time onto Dumbass' face. She became a flurry of black dots, jumping and streaming venom, dive bombing Walter's savior with vicious kisses.

Dumbass screeched and shouted, swatted and jumped, but to no avail. He bobbed in and out of Walter's view, each time looking more bloated and sick. For a long time, Walter watched the blue sky above him. Screams gave way to whimpers and pleas, then silence and the occasional rasping gasp. Then Dumbass slumped into Walter's eye line for one final, slow hour. His face grew redder and his limbs began to swell and pale as his body wilted just out of sight.

Walter heard a thud. With all his might, he managed to move his eye one millimeter to the left. As he glared in horror at the corpse of his liberator lying next to him, the Spider danced back onto Walter's eye and began—patiently, serenely—to preen herself.

death in the living room

By Joan Doyle

The day is appointed and time is propelling me toward it so fast it is taking my breath away. It is inevitable, agreed upon by all concerned, even if for some it is causing deep sadness and some confusion. I move through my childhood home as if in a dream. My family seems to move silently, solemnly around me. I take my pilgrimage to all the familiar rooms, savoring memories and feeling full with the richness of a life which began within these walls. I have traveled far into strange and wonderful places but none meant more to me than this place. It's where I come to in my dreams, where my mind, before words could articulate assent or refusal, took on the complex journey the years were to unfold. Now it is to conclude.

As people gather at the chapel I feel emotions collide within me; fear of leaving the known for the void. What dreams may come, I can not know but I have to go. It is my time. I look around and the simple joys of this life call to me, begging me to stay and savor just one more day of earthy pleasures. The winter sun sending slanting beams through rain-filled clouds is a watercolor I will never paint. The air crisp against my face makes my skin tingle and the blood coursing through my veins fights to keep me warm. My nose and cheeks glowing rosy even as my wide-staring eyes look death in the face. I must be strong; we all must leave some day.

Among the crowd gathering, I see a press reporter and feel anger at the intrusion on this most sacred day. Someone needs to do something about these people. It shouldn't have to be me. I need to be quiet, to really let go of all attachment, to enter into that place I know in meditation. There I feel the peace that comes with that blissful diffusion of the boundaries of skin; nothing to fight against, nothing to fight for. All is as it should be. What does it matter, I think. Let them come. Let them record the first death by appointment in this part of the world. I'm out of here, what do I care? Then I look to my family and anger rises up again. Their sadness needs to be respected.

My entourage gathers about me and I am ushered into the sanctuary. Inside the chapel I feel the agitation of my own mixed emotions and the anticipation of the crowd. There is no peace here. I see those officiating gathered near the altar. This is a serious matter and the gravity is reflected in their faces. I see the glass-covered casket lying in wait and a part of me calms to know how efficient it will be. I will get inside and once it is sealed I break the capsule and the gas does its work in seconds; painless, like falling asleep under anesthetic. Then that will be all she wrote! End of story.

My human mind bounces to the known and all that is to be left behind; my thoughts race. Did I make the most of every day? Is there more to do? Memories flash, blinding my eyes and ears to the drone of the ceremony beginning. I am lost in sunny days and loved faces and what ifs. My heart is pulling me back, as if from a precipice, my primal survival instinct railing against extinction. My vision returns and I look at some of the faces around me. I want them to know this feeling, to know what it feels like to be standing on the brink of oblivion; to have run out of time. They have not run out of time. Do they realize their good fortune? Are they celebrating the life within them, are they living life fully?

I am seized by this idea and suddenly I am yanking the microphone from the startled priest's hands and speaking manically to the rapt crowd. "Before I go I think I deserve to speak my mind," I say. "This day is my end," I shout, "but it's not yours. You may have days or years yet to enjoy this earth. How I envy you. Grab your time with both hands. Life is an experiment. Don't live a small and limited life, take risks. If you only knew the fleetingness of this lifetime, you would live big, love big. You are more amazing than you know. I have no time left but I see so clearly now the incredible gift that life is."

I realize then with expanding ferocity that I don't want to die. I am enraptured with this clarity and I scream it out even as I run for the door, "I don't want to die!" I burst out into the bracing air. I run and run with this energy of vibrant life within me, feeling delight in my physical body, my heart pumping, my thighs aching, my face tingling with the cold, my breath visible before me. I run all the way home. I go to the heart of the house seeking the open fire in the living room. All of my senses are scintillating. Everything gives me pleasure—the heat, the light pink glow of the walls, the colorful photos of smiling family faces—I am alive, I am alive.

Just then I become aware of a cool liquid in my hand. In my passion I have squeezed the capsule the priest placed there. I fling it to the ground. The vapor begins to fill the air. I am seized by panic and I escape the room slamming the door behind me. I hear my family now trickling into the house making their way toward me, shedding coats and scarves and speaking in cheery tones. I stand with my hand on the doorknob. "Don't go in there," I say. "There's death in the living room."

death room

By Matt McGinnis

My friend Tommy tried to convince me the noise was just my landlady's cat. For a few nights I held onto the notion, though I was never completely convinced. Cats don't scratch their paws along walls late at night as spitefully as what I had been hearing. They also don't scratch the plaster from halfway up the ceiling to the floor. It was always coming from the other side of my bedroom wall, always in the same location.

I was renting a small guestroom in an old woman's house while I searched for steady work. The woman's name was Susie, and I guessed she was in her late eighties by her deep wrinkles, dyed hair, and hanging jowls. My bedroom was cramped but serviceable, though it wasn't long before I noticed that Susie never left the house. Not for anything.

Susie's only rule was that I was not to enter her husband's room under any circumstance, despite his having died years ago. In the brief glimpses I'd had into the room, I saw that his personal belongings remained intact, including portraits, photos, antiques, his acoustic guitar, and some of his hand-written notes. I was told that her husband had died in that very room, on a wooden rocking chair that still stood in the far corner. This was the room where the scratching came from. The wall behind my bedpost was adjacent to it.

I called this room the death room.

Several weeks into my stay, I began hearing objects fall in the death room. Plates crashed to the floor and books fell from shelves. I took comfort in the notion that it was the cat. That is, until I woke to a shattering plate while the cat slept by my feet.

Then the voices came. It was always the hoarse whisper of an old man, calling my name, beckoning me into that room. Finally I decided to confront my own fear and put my imagination to rest. One night I ventured into the hallway and saw that the death room's door was wide open. I crept into the shadows as I heard steady breathing from all around me. In the darkness, two bloodshot eyes stared back at me. Then, a voice called out, interrupting my investigation.

"Get out!" it barked. I whirled around and peered through the doorway. In the living room was the outline of Susie, sitting on her couch, drenched in darkness. "That room is off limits," she continued. The shadows made her appear dreadful. I nodded and returned to my bedroom. How long had she been staring into that open door?

I had nowhere else to go that I could afford, and part of me was drawn to the strange mystery surrounding the death room. I suppose that's what kept me from moving. When met with the possibility of proving life after death, I found, the curiosity surmounts the fear, no matter how awful the answer.

I waited one night until well past two in the morning. My chances of seeing something were best at night, and Susie would be asleep by then. I sipped coffee throughout the night to keep me alert. The familiar scratching had started moments before I went exploring. It was as though it anticipated my arrival.

In the hallway I saw that the death room's door was shut. I opened it, and the door creaked too loud for comfort. I didn't want to wake Susie. Since the night she caught me inside the death room, I suspected she had a dark side, a fiery hatred for all things living, well hidden by her innocent smile. Since that night, I wondered if she wanted me dead.

In the death room, the rocking chair swung back and forth wildly. Plates were shattered over the floor. The room was rank, as though it had been holding a decomposed body for ages. I did my best not to vomit. I walked deeper into the room, when a voice whispered from beside me. I could feel its ice-cold breath hit my neck. I turned toward it, but saw nothing.

Then, in the periphery of my vision, I saw it through the mirror. An old man with the face of Susie's dead husband stared back at me.

Get out, his voice whispered, though his lips never moved. *Get out while you can...*

There was no malice in his voice. Rather, it sounded pleading. Then, another light breath hit my neck. I was terrified to turn around, but I slowly did, and found myself suddenly face to face with Susie.

At invisible force whipped the carpet completely off the floor. I tripped over it, went sprawling, and looked up to see Susie glaring down at me. With the carpet gone, the stone floor around me was decorated with ancient, arcane symbols. Susie hoisted an open palm at the mirror, and I saw the image of her husband fade away. Had he only been trying to warn me?

Suddenly the lines in Susie's skin began to fill in, and color returned to her wispy white hair. I looked down and saw that the flesh on my own arms was aging considerably and becoming desiccated. It was then that I noticed something horrible in the photos. Judging by the garb, they were taken too long ago to be Susie's husband. They were from colonial America.

How long had Susie been alive, and was I just another young man in a long line of victims?

Shadows danced around me, and Susie's jaw stretched down to an unnatural length as it devoured my life. The symbols spanning the floor glowed a hellish scarlet.

Floating in the death room, I looked down at my wizened, lifeless body as it crumbled into ash. A young and beautiful Susie shut me in the room's darkness. I don't know how long I've been trapped here with the countless others she killed, but I'm determined to save the next victim.

the dog

By Cynthia Lyons

In the dark, I watch. I know it's that damn dog! I had to clean the *window* in the basement again. It seems to be constantly covered over with dirt. That flea bag probably kicks it up in front of the window after eating my tulips and taking a dump in my *flower* bed.

Of course, Nancy is going to do nothing. I wanted to shoot it, but the wife says, "No, that's not nice!"

It's only because she doesn't care about the lawn like I do. We've been married for over forty years, and she has never cared about the lawn like I have. I guess I'll figure it out myself. One of these days, I'm going to have to get a light down here.

I went to the store yesterday. I don't want something that people will know it was me. I have to constantly yell at that foul creature to get the hell out of my yard. Still, Nancy does nothing, and I know she watches from her kitchen window while that mutt goes out to do its business.

"Earl? Come get your dinner! I'm not going to keep it warm for you all night!"

I go upstairs and sit at the table, imagining the aromatic browned roast is actually that little brown crap machine next door. As I carve slices off, I imagine I can actually hear it whining, begging for mercy when it is slid into the oven.

After dinner, I go back down to the basement. I know there is a way to take care of this problem, I just need to think. I could just wait until dark and set out a dish of antifreeze and hamburger meat. The vomiting alone would kill it. Except, with my luck, the rotten mongrel would toss its insides all over my lawn. I would be cleaning intestines and green hamburger out of my *flowers* for weeks to come! I will probably pick it up when no one is around and drop it on a back road somewhere. There is fun in watching it suffer, I can readily admit. I have been missing things lately though. I feel as if I am splitting into two different minds. Things have been missing from my box.

Nancy says someone shaved the mutt's behind the other day and now there is nasty brown hair all over my basement floor. I wish I remembered doing it, I imagine it was exciting to watch the animal squirm. I need to get this dog problem taken care of soon; I fear it will push me over the edge if I don't. My wife says people have seen me at places I know I would never go to willingly. There is something going on in my mind and I know it is the dog's fault. Five years of watching it traipse happily through my yard, stopping to do whatever it is that those mongrels do, no one caring, all of them laughing—telling me I'm paranoid and I worry too much–it has finally done me in.

I woke up this morning to the sound of Nancy shrieking next door. My wife had run out the door in her dressing gown, eager to be of help to a friend in need. Such a concerned woman, my wife.

It appears the dog had an accident in the night. From what I could make out from the hysterical women, it went like this: Nancy awoke this morning to a horrible smell and stickiness on the sheets beside her. She opened her eyes to see what it was and found the head of her precious poochie. There were splashes of blood all over her bedroom walls but nowhere else. They think the head may have been thrown in through the window. I want to say how difficult it was to throw that far and high...instead I say nothing except to offer my flower bed as the final resting spot. Maybe the dog could be useful yet.

eyes of the beholder

By Hal Kempka

Dirk searched the Village Green part of town, and finally found the Art Cosmos gallery. The flier promoting a new artist's work called it a place for those drawn to the *avant-garde* and unusual. It sat off the main drag in a darkened alley, with a single 60-watt light bulb illuminating the sign over the door.

When he stepped inside, the room quieted momentarily. The throng of guests cast a quick, disapproving stare at the new arrival before resuming their conversations. Dirk passed them off as a bunch of weirdos in gaudy make up and somber, Gothic clothing that appeared more appropriate for a funeral rather than an art showing.

Felicia, the drag queen owner, greeted him like he was an old friend, giving him a quick hug and an air kiss on the cheek.

"Welcome to my gallery, you handsome devil. I've not seen you here before, so please sign my guestbook; I do want to know who you are."

After a waiter brought her and Dirk a glass of wine, Felicia strode off to flit amongst the crowd. Dirk followed the critics and patrons through a series of maze-like room dividers.

They stopped and studied each painting, entranced by the ostensible interaction of surreal relief and sculpture. The crimson signature read "Carmella."

Several patrons referred to her collection as exquisite, entrancing, bizarre, chilling, and frighteningly attractive. He thought it nearer to "chillingly bizarre."

"Do you like my work?"

The deep, sultry voice in the shadows startled him. Dirk spun around, spilling wine on his jacket. A gaunt-faced woman lingered on the fringe of the darkened corner.

"Oh! I didn't see you standing there," he said, dabbing the spill with his napkin. "And to answer your question: yes, I do. It is quite out of the ordinary."

"I didn't mean to startle you," she said, brushing a shock of auburn hair away from her face. "I'm Carmella, the so-called honored artist. And thank you—I think—for that compliment."

Her dilated eyes burned through him in an intense stare. *What an odd duck*, he thought, though he felt immediately attracted to her. She said it was her first professional showing, and that Felicia had billed it as Carmella's "coming out" party.

She felt uncomfortable being in the limelight, and feared her work would be deemed amateurish. She worried patrons would not appreciate the passion she put into each piece, so she decided to watch and listen to comments without being seen.

Her stomach emitted a hungry growl. "Well," he said, "You sound starved. Can I get you some *hors d'oeuvres*?"

He brought her a small plate of cheese and crackers, and she led him from painting to painting. Each one represented something of the human condition. The *papier-mâché* body parts and everyday implements conveyed that people were expendable resources, no different than the everyday trash they discarded.

Her work both attracted and repulsed the patrons. Dirk noticed "sold" tags taped to several pieces.

An eight-by-ten-foot painting titled "Blame" showed arrows aimed at acrylic fingers pointing outward. She chuckled when a visitor, standing in a finger's line of sight, shivered and quickly stepped aside.

In her piece, *The Big Bang*, swirling kaleidoscopic colors exploded across the canvas from variously sized pistols. Deep red blotches of crimson enamel ran down the canvas from the bas-reliefs of shattered, textured faces.

Blinded Visions, however, drew the largest crowd. Broken eyeglasses and fluorescent eyeballs filled the black-light-illuminated, midnight-blue canvas. Silvery tears dripped from a single pair of bright blue eyes that appeared to stare directly at the observer.

"My God," a woman whispered as they walked past. "I can't imagine what the artist was thinking, but this is brilliant."

Carmella squeezed Dirk's arm, barely containing her smile. As the showing came to a close, Felicia introduced Carmella to the gallery crowd. Her timid stance broadened and her head rose erect when cheers and applause filled the room.

When well-wishers and hangers-on swarmed her, Dirk saw that she began to hyperventilate. He seized the opportunity and dragged her away from the crowd.

Walking her to her car, Dirk said, "Carmella, I am very attracted to you and would like to see you again."

She smiled, and gave him a peck on the cheek. "Then, why don't you follow me home and we can get to know each other better."

A half-hour out of town, Carmella took a long dirt drive to a secluded cabin. The night air's sharp balsam scent refreshed him as he stepped from the car. She led him past the house, and into her studio: a large shed where she stayed while working on a new project.

"Don't you ever find the seclusion daunting?" he asked.

Carmella laughed and disappeared into another room. She returned shortly, carrying two glasses of wine. They sat on a couch, and he offered a toast to her success.

She then snuggled against him and rested her head against his chest.

"Your heartbeat is so strong," she said. "It sounds like it could beat forever."

Minutes later, however, Dirk felt his heart slowing. His breathing turned labored and his eyes blurred. As he drifted in and out of consciousness, Carmella rolled a splattered paint canvas across the floor.

She stroked his pale cheek and dragged him off the couch. Dirk felt a deep burning in his chest. He lay unable to move, though he twitched for a few seconds while she drew a scalpel down his chest and over his belly.

The following morning, Carmella hurried to her studio and assembled her new supply of materials. She retrieved the gurney from the walk-in freezer containing Dirk's cold, partially dissected corpse.

She dipped his slit-in-half and *papier-mâché*'d heart in acrylic resin, and centered it on the canvas. Carmella placed his eyes between the left and right aortas, and stood back to admire her new piece: *Love at First Sight*.

the fall from glory

By Alyssa Cooper

It's cold in the city tonight. I walk with my hands deep in my pockets, although I can't feel the chill. I haven't felt anything so trivial in a very long time. I'm much stronger than that.

I'm a stalker, a feline, a shadowy coat with black spots. I move through the city like a panther in the forest, climbing concrete trees. The humans here are my prey, reeking of fear that they don't yet comprehend. I follow them, moving slowly, tasting the air. I could overpower them, take them down with long teeth and hands clenched like claws. I could pound them to the earth and hold them while they screamed in my sensitive, twitching ears.

But I can't do that. It would never satisfy. I'm a stalker; this is not as simple as being a hunter. I follow, twisting through the streets and ducking into alleys. With her scent in my nostrils, I don't need to see her. I can feel her inside. My prey is a part of me.

The cold can't turn me from the hunt. It is one on a long list of the things that can no longer inconvenience me: poison, drowning, blades, flames, guns. Death in general. I'm immortal now, as I should be. How would the prey react if they saw their stalker shudder?

Tonight, she is young and blonde. Her arms are thin but her face is round and her thighs are thick. She smells strongly of herself. I prefer human women now the way that I preferred them when I was one myself; the sweet taste of their soft skin and their heartbeats fluttering between their collarbones. Their meek hands grabbing for me in lust and excitement as their painted lips part in a gasp. Stalking is a lot like flirting. Killing is a lot like conquest.

We traverse the city. She walks with tight, tiny steps, and I follow languidly. I let her hear my footsteps. Glimpse my shadow. I can smell her fear, thick, like a cloud of sultry pink trailing behind her. My mouth waters.

I play the game until I can hear her heart slamming with fear, until she breathes with ragged gasps and she looks over her shoulder at every turn. Until she corners herself in the dark. Only then do I let myself be seen.

I step out of an alley, into her view, and her fear melts sluggishly. It's not just my unthreatening, feminine stature. I'm beautiful; I'm alluring. She can't help but be hypnotized.

She already loves me.

She doesn't falter as I step forward. She doesn't flinch when I reach for her shoulders. I pull her and she comes willingly, pressing her body against mine as I wrap my arms around her. When I bury my face in her neck, I'm blinded by the stench, and she moans in sweet ecstasy. My lips part. My teeth caress her skin before they break the surface, and she gasps, lost.

She clings to me, clutching like a lover... but when I get too excited, I lose my concentration. The illusion slips. Her eyes are no longer blind when she opens them again; she feels pain, and starts to scream.

This is the climax. This is better than orgasm. I grab her hair and her soft skin, tearing, my fingernails leaving long trails of blood. She screams louder, fighting against me, but

I'm the hunter here. I easily hold her valiant efforts. I bite down harder. I drink deeper. I drink until her heart skips and stutters. Her fists are round and soft as she beats me. Like little pillows. And then she is limp.

I drink for a long time after her heart stops, and when I'm finished, I let her body fall without ceremony. She crumples at my feet, facedown and graceless. I wipe my lips and lick my teeth, savouring the last taste. Perfect.

When I turn to leave, there is a man blocking my path. My hackles rise instantly; I should have heard him approach. How did he get so close? He smiles at me.

He is more monstrous than I am, less human. If I am a jaguar, he is a hulking tiger, stretching tall above me and baring incomparable teeth. For the first time in an age, I feel prickling fear. I take a step back, but he lifts one hand, and I can't help but stop. There's something captivating in his eyes. They're so wide...so dark.

He comes towards me slowly, and I tense, but for some reason I can't run. He's upon me in an instant, wrapping me up in his arms. His red lips come close, filling up my vision. He opens his mouth, and where I have two elegant fangs, he has four. I know what's happening, but my mind can't comprehend the dire consequences. It's been so long since I've been completely consumed.

He lowers his face to my throat. I feel his breath, and I can't help but moan as it ignites my skin. His grip on me tightens; his mouth is sealed on my flesh. Time stands still in his sweet embrace.

Finally, the voice in my head is loud enough to understand: *you're going to die.* Sluggishly, I start to struggle. I ball my fists and strike, but my blows go unnoticed. I try to scream, but his bite is too tight—and then it tightens. This is his orgasm; I recognize the excitement. The pain stabs through my body as he sucks harder and harder, as if he's trying to turn me inside out. It's too late. I don't have the strength.

I think of the blonde girl's blood, running hot down my throat. It will be hotter in his.

The city swings up around me, and then I'm staring at the stars. They swell brilliantly, eating up the darkness. He's standing over me. Wiping his lips. But I only see the stars.

the farmer in the dell

By Diane Spodarek

She was always playing the piano. Always playing the piano. Instead of feeding the chickens, she was playing the piano. And at night she went to the bar and played the piano with him. So I threw her out. Her and the piano. She's with him now. Piano's in the duck pond.

She called and said she wants to come over and get her stuff. Sure, I said, come on over. I'm waiting for her, having a cup of tea, got the twelve-gauge ready. Should I say, "Cup of tea, love?" before or after? After might be funnier.

farmer john

By Philip Murray-Lawson

"Do we really have to go through with it?" Hayley's mother asks.

"It's the deal," her father replies.

"Haven't we given enough?"

Hayley's father hunches further over the wheel and, despite the rain that sweeps in relentless curtains across the motorway, squeezes the accelerator. The car speeds on, its headlamps illuminating gray barriers and the glistening tarmac. Theirs is the only vehicle on the road.

"We owe him everything," he says. Hayley has often heard her parents speak about how hard life is since the collapse of the Euro Zone. Subventions have dwindled to nothing and farmers are finding it harder and harder to eke out a living. Every day, her father reads aloud reports of bankruptcies from the newspapers. She remembers her mother's distress at the suicide of a neighbour. But Hayley's parents have found a way to survive. And even prosper. They have followed old-fashioned, primitive methods. Their friends mocked at first, but now they are intrigued and jealous. Hayley is aware of this as a child is—without fully comprehending.

"She's just seven years old," her mother says. Hayley realizes that they have been talking about her. Despite the drag of her seatbelt, she leans closer, but her parents no longer speak. Beside her, Louise, her younger sister, has been alternately singing little songs or dozing. Hayley likes to listen to her, but now there is only the sound of shallow breathing. It is too dark to see her face; and when Hayley holds her own white hands out in front of her, she can hardly see them either. Her parents' heads are shadowy carvings on the top of a wall. She wonders why she feels so anxious. The journey from their home in Cardiff has been going on forever. She takes a deep breath. The air is warm and smells of crisps, orange juice, and plastic. After a while, she is once more lulled by the hum of the motor, the electronic blips from the dashboard, and the tap, tap, tap of the rain. She closes her eyes.

"She might not see him," her father says. "If she doesn't see him, we don't have to... Not this year." The car is swerving off the motorway. Hayley glimpses low stone walls and furrowed earth. A skeletal tree on the horizon waves tortured branches. The moon has risen, and drifts among dispersing clouds. Her father's back curves, his face approaches the windscreen, he heaves on the wheel and the tires swish through water sending a huge wave into the ditch. A hare is trapped wild and shy in a flood of yellow. Her father gives a low whistle, straightens the trajectory, and stretches back in his seat. The car accelerates onwards. It seems that the dawn will never come.

Hayley curls over onto her side; she shuts her eyes tightly, but cannot sleep; the atmosphere has changed. Although, the car shows no signs of slowing, she has that edgy, journey's end feeling. She sits up, peering through the raindrops at the featureless fields. The moon is stark and cold.

A man, seated on a horse-drawn cart, gazes in at her through the car window. He is wearing a dark suit, a straw hat, and holds the reins loosely in luminous fingers. His ochre face is round and hairless, its surface pitted with craters. It swells and contracts in the moonlight. The man knows that Hayley has seen him. He grins and raises a rusty sickle. Hayley starts back. The horse and cart keep pace with her, floating impossibly above the roadside.

"Mummy," Hayley cries. "There's a man outside! He has a horse!"

She feels her parents stiffen. Despite her fear, she realises that she has said something wrong. She shuts her mouth.

"Farmer John," her mother whispers. "She's seen him."

"We're here," Hayley's father says. He turns left, and parks by an open gate. Other cars are already there. Hayley stares about her, but the man on the cart has disappeared.

"We'll leave Louise here," her father says. Hayley's parents clamber from their seats.

"Come on, Hayley," her mother says. Doors slam. Hayley stands in the mud, her breath billowing. Her father lifts her into his arms, and walks through the damp grasses. They hiss around his ankles. Her mother hesitates, and then follows. Hayley can see other parents; there appear to be dozens of them; they too are carrying children. She recognises some of them. No one speaks. They are all converging on the center of the field.

The horse and cart are there. There is also a black, ancient stone. The man in the dark suit and straw hat is waiting for them. His blood-stained sickle is raised in the moonlight.

fifty years

By Debbie Lampi

Mangy dogs yap outside the cyclone fence. The bougainvillea that Abuelo planted has purple papery blossoms as fine as rice paper, and climbs the chain-linked fence. Its spiny thorns are tipped with a black, waxy substance, further protection against intruders. The bird-of-paradise plants' bright claw-like blossoms bloom alongside the palms. They would dry and desiccate like old bones in this heat if my grandmother did not spend hours tending them. A faded pink flamingo has toppled over in the yard and I reach to right it.

Ornate iron bars painted black cover the doors and windows of their tiny stucco house. The North Miami suburb has become a hardscrabble neighborhood. I ring the doorbell and get no response. I ring again and notice that the gate is ajar, swinging on its hinges. The heavy teak door opens easily as I push. My grandmother's glasses are on the floor, the glass crushed, the wire frames crumpled like tin foil.

I call my grandparents as I enter, "*Abuela, Abuelo, soy yo, Jorge!*" On June thirtieth, *mis abuelos* will celebrate fifty years together and I've come to help plan the celebration. *Abuelo* must have forgotten to lock the door after he picked up the morning paper. The small table where *Abuelo* lays his keys is lying on its side, its contents spilled next to the morning edition. Its headlines scream, *"Crime Rate Soars!"* in bold print.

The interior is cool and dim, and yet a trickle of perspiration runs along my upper lip. The pungent odor of fried fish hangs heavy in the air. *Abuela* has been cooking. ChiChi, their prized Macaw, screeches, *"Buenos Días, Buenos Días!"* over and over again. ChiChi's strong curved bill and her claws make her a fierce competitor for *Abuela's* affection; seeing me, she becomes agitated and tears at her bright green tail feathers. She begins to rattle her cage and screeches, "No, Rey, no! No, Rey, no!"

"Quiet, ChiChi," I yell. I want to turn and run, to flee the raucous screeching.

"*Abuela?*" I call.

My grandmother is a Cuban grandmother—always delighted to see me, ready with a suffocating hug to her ample bosom, an *"Ay bendito, Jorge*—Where have you been?" and a big *besito.*

"*Abuelo?* Anybody home?" I call as I walk toward the bright, airy kitchen. The only sound is the ticking of the grandfather clock my grandparents bought in honor of their anniversary.

I tread softly and hold my breath as I push open the kitchen door.

"*Abuela?*"

Grandmother's crystal goblets and cloth napkins adorn the kitchen table. I breathe a sigh of relief. Lunch for two. A cauldron of rice and beans sits on top of the white enamel stove. A pitcher of ice water drips cool, clear, liquid beads on the counter top. The lunch plates have been scraped and set in the sink to soak. I hear voices but it is only the sound of *Abuela's* small television on the kitchen counter. It is turned to the news at noon, the commentator's seductive voice as silky as satin. An old tattered edition of Ernest Hemingway's *The Old Man and the Sea* sits on top of the counter. I flip it open, and in my grandmother's elegant and precise penmanship, the inscription reads:

29 June 1960
To My Co-Captain: A small token of love and devotion to the man I couldn't imagine sailing the world without. No matter what the sailing conditions, it is you I will stand side-by-side with. Forever and always.
Your fellow Co-Captain, Cookie

ChiChi's shrieking and the news commentator's seductive voice have masked a soft gurgling sound like water over stones. I follow the sound to the guest bathroom. The avocado toilet and tub, and the antique white cabinets, are badly in need of renovation. I glance at my face in the splotchy mirror, which is mounted in a faux-antique gold frame. I am wide-eyed, my pupils black in my pale face. I am breathing rapidly. The toilet is running, and I stop to jiggle the handle. The house has a smell of old people and Aspercreme.

I follow the gurgling sound to my grandparents' room. The door is open. I first notice the ceiling fan rotating lackadaisically. And then I notice *Abuela*. She lies in stillness— her ruffled peach bed cover has been carefully folded at the bottom of the bed for her afternoon siesta. I stare at her in horror. Her nap has been interrupted by the squalor of death. A gaping wound weeps at her temple. Her face is in repose; her eyelids are ominous and heavy. Already her skin has a waxy pallor. Her arms lie by her sides, plump and composed, as if death came peacefully. Fear gnaws at my stomach; an acrid taste rises to my throat as I begin to scream.

Abuelo knows no such peace. An ugly, heavy, black firearm lies on the floor, mere inches from his struggling form. The wound to his chest is angry. Bright red blood cascades into his crisp white collar. His life is slowly ebbing right out of this world.

"*Abuelo!*" I yell as I rush to his side. "What happened?"

He raises his head and makes one last effort to push himself up. He looks at me before he says, "I was not her co-captain," and then collapses onto the cold terrazzo tile.

the fox and the rain

By Adam Millard

I arrived on Halcyon Drive to the satisfying noise of rising birds. It was still dark, and I found myself wondering whether this could have waited until morning. The drive was ominously lit with staggered lamps; beneath one of them an inquisitive fox riffled through the remains of overturned rubbish. Strangely—and this only further fueled my sudden sense of unease—it didn't rush away at the sight of me approaching. Instead, it cocked an ear and made a horrific mewling noise before returning to the pile of empty milk-cartons and stripped chicken bones scattered haphazardly along the curb.

One of the houses suddenly lit up, and I could see a silhouetted figure traipsing around beyond the curtains. I wondered if the occupants of the house had been roused by the fox's reprehensible keen, or whether they had seen me arrive and were in the process of calling the police. Either way, I didn't care. I had been summoned to Halcyon Drive, not of my own accord, but on behalf of my transcendental dreams, which were never to be ignored.

In the dream, everything was as it appeared now. The rows of houses perfectly aligned with immaculately maintained gardens; the bicycle-path—on which I now stood—

stretching the length of the road; even the monotonously chirruping birds sitting atop the hundred-year-old oak trees which would block out the sun, I estimated, from the hours of three until five of a Summer's afternoon. The only aberration was the fox; that had *not* been part of the reverie, which was altogether unsettling, for I had never envisioned anything additional since the dreams began.

The shadow beyond the curtain moved from left to right, and the light went out once again. I couldn't shake the idea that the residents were all watching me, now; a stranger on their turf. In the spaghetti-westerns of yesteryear, I would have been the man without a name, the protagonist arriving just in time to a gunfight. I listened carefully for the sounds of wooden shutters being slammed and bolted, but was met with only silence and the sound of a tin-can being pushed nervously along the ground by the nose of the fox.

I walked with some temerity along the path; the fox mewled once again—as was its wont—and began to chew frantically on a piece of crusty bread peppered with the grotesque blue and green spots of week-old decay. It shouldn't be there, I told myself. It doesn't belong....

A few drops of rain splashed my shoulders, and then it came harder; a torrential downpour that belonged just as much as the misplaced fox.

What was happening? This was all...*wrong*. The dreams were never wrong, which was what caused the hackles to rise on the nape of my neck and gooseflesh to appear beneath my dampening clothes. The fox and the rain were disheartening anomalies, mystifying me with their presence. I wanted to run, to race away from Halcyon Drive without glancing back. And yet I couldn't. My legs felt coagulated, as if the bones had been removed and replaced with something viscous and fluid. I could barely walk, now, and the fox was staring at me, knowingly.

I could swear it smiled at me.

I composed myself, brushed the sodden hair away from my forehead. Somewhere, off in the distance, I heard sirens. Plural, flying through the semi-darkness in perfect unison. My heart sped, staccato bursts threatening to erupt within me. The silhouette had called the police, after all, reporting a strange man standing out on their Utopian boulevard, a man who had brought with him—for some unknown reason—a hungry fox and a rainstorm.

The sirens drew nearer; the fox sat back on its haunches. The only thing missing was its popcorn.

I urged myself to move, and my recalcitrant legs finally obeyed. I made my way past the fox—smiling?—and past the house belonging to the silhouette. Crossing the road, I quickened my pace; jellied legs beneath me, as if I had recently competed in marathons I had no warrant to enter.

I was halfway across the road when the deafening sirens raucously pulled onto Halcyon drive. I turned, held my hands up in surrender, for I hadn't done anything wrong...not really. It was then that I saw the black car, but only for a split-second. I think it hit me, though all I could see were stars, concrete, stars, concrete, smiling fox, concrete....

The sirens hadn't been for me; a high-speed chase—*a group of drunken youths in the black car*—had led the police to Halcyon Drive. Talk about unfortunate. And as I lay on my back, staring up the length of a hundred-year-old oak, blood seeping from my shattered skull and painting the crusty-brown fallen leaves an undesirable hue of crimson, I knew that things would have turned out very differently if it hadn't been for that hungry fox, for that inappropriately-timed shower.

I closed my eyes and listened to the birdsong, for I had nothing else to do.

a game of tag

By Paul Stansbury

I remember that house, perched up there on the creek bank. The third window from the left, low to the ground, was my room. We had no air conditioning then. On hot summer nights, a rusty screen that could hardly resist the thumps of moths was all that kept what lurked outside from coming in. My bed lay under the window to catch the occasional breeze. The curtains would draw in and then press out against the screen as if the whole house was taking a deep breath.

I remember the night noises along the creek bank. Katydids, loud and raucous, joined the chirping of crickets to fill the darkness with a plaintive ballad. The deep baritone calls of bullfrogs rolled up the steep bank. The soft, splitting sound of the creek, as it flowed around the huge pock-marked boulder which sat defiantly in its path, floated through the heavy air. This discordant symphony would coalesce into a driving rhythm, as if the night was suddenly frightened: making its heart beat wildly. Then, as quickly as the crescendo reached its apex, all fell silent at the sound of a breaking twig, the rustle of dead leaves, or an unfamiliar splash in the creek's murky water.

I remember waiting in the silence: waiting for it to come up to my window. I knew it lurked in the dark, muddy water in a hole beneath that rock. I knew it subsisted on the cold-blooded creatures that slithered in the mud on the creek bottom. I also knew it hungered in the dark for the warm, soft flesh of children.

Slowly, silently, it would make its way up the bank under the cover of the sounds of the night, stopping only when the symphony was interrupted. I waited. If I were completely still, completely silent, it couldn't find me. If I moved or made a sound, I knew it would tear through the flimsy screen and rip my body apart; stuffing the bloody pulp into its gaping maw, licking the gore from its bony claws.

I remember lying there in the stifling heat night after night, drawing the covers up over my head, not moving. It couldn't smell me, it couldn't see me if I had the covers pulled over my head. Each breath was measured, taking an eternity, so that the movement of my chest could not be detected. It was like diving down to the bottom of the pool and holding your breath until your lungs almost burst trying to swim to the top; but on these endless summer nights, I had to stay perfectly still. On the hottest nights, the sweat trickled along my neck but still I couldn't move. My lungs would ache for just one, long, cool draft of air, but I didn't dare pull the covers down. Not while it lurked outside. I lay completely still, no movement to give me away.

Some nights I couldn't tell where it lurked, but I kept my covers pulled up tight. Other nights I knew it was crouching right outside my window. Those nights I wanted to leap out of the bed to run and hide, but I knew it would be too quick. I knew it would catch me. Through those terrifying summer nights, we played this cat-and-mouse game.

I remember the night I awoke to silence. A cool breeze drifted over me and the soft fresh night air filled my lungs. I had only a single moment to enjoy it before I realized in horror that I had kicked the covers off and left myself exposed. It was then that I felt the drop of water fall on my face.

I looked up into its pale eyes, looming only inches from my face. One cold, wet hand slammed down hard on my chest pinning me to the bed, while the other grasped my head pushing it down into my pillow. I wanted to scream out for help; but my heart, filled with terror, pounded my throat closed and beat the air from my lungs. Large, flat, eyes drifted closer to my face. A dank breath poured down, stinging my cheeks like an icy blast on a winter's day. As those weeping eyes drew close, I saw the universe of black desolation within.

I remember the pain, like the time I burned my hand on the stove, but everywhere in my body and all at once. Then blackness, stillness.

I opened my eyes to see a child in bed. I was holding it down with ruthless hands. Drawing back, I gazed at the oddly familiar face. I shivered in the cloying night air. That child was me! I retched with the sudden and overwhelming realization that my body had been taken. I stood there for a long time, confused and terrified. I wanted my body back, but I knew it no longer belonged to me. Then, the sleeping child that had been me pulled the covers up. A smile, like the taunting smirk of a child having just tagged a playmate "It," spread across his beaming face.

Resigned to my fate, I slipped out of the window and back down to the creek where I found a hole under the rock.

That was many years ago. Since then, I have dined on the cold flesh of the small beasts that slither on the bottom of the creek. I have waited here in the cold and murky water.

I remember. I will keep an eye on that house. Someday, a child will sleep in that room again. I will wait, and when the katydids and crickets sing on a summer's night, I will creep up to that window and if that child is not careful, I will have a warm bed to sleep in once again.

general anesthesia

By John R. Mabry

She looked frail to him, standing beside her locker. He walked up behind her and said, "Hey, Clare." She jumped. When she saw it was him, she relaxed. She moved her hand over the back of her neck, and grabbed at the tie of her scrubs.

Dan was glad to see her, but it shook him to see her...like this. "I'm glad you're back," he said. She looked at the ground and mumbled, "Thanks."

He didn't know the details. He wasn't sure he wanted to. The word was, she'd been attacked, but what did that mean? In his mind's eye he saw her beat up and bloodied, but deeper violations were possible. He'd heard that they got the guy, but they had to kill him to take him down. There was so much he wanted to know, but it didn't look like Clare wanted to talk.

She started down the hall, and he fell into pace alongside her. "Clare, I don't mean to pry, but...are you sure you're ready to come back?"

"No, I'm not," she said, and her answer surprised him. He'd never known anyone tougher than her. If he could choose anyone to be beside him in an alley fight, it wouldn't be Joe Carroll, the enormous, burly nurse in Oncology—it would be *her*. "But I don't think *you're* going to pay my rent." She was right—after his student loans, he could barely pay his own.

"Anything I need to know?" she asked. They paused just outside the scrub room for privacy.

"We've pretty much switched to Moxflurane for most procedures. I did my first patient with it about the time you...of your accident. Did you ever...?"

She shook her head. "No, but I've read all the literature. It's pretty much the same as Enflurane, right?" She was referring to the drug that, until recently, they'd used for most surgeries requiring general anesthesia.

"Yeah, but there's something the lit doesn't tell you."

"What's that?"

"It makes them talk," Dan smiled. He remembered a couple of humdingers.

"A lot of them talk," she countered.

"But this is deep stuff—you know how the neuroses come out of the closet with Enfluerane? That's nothing compared to this stuff."

"Well, this could be fun," she flashed a weak smile. It didn't last long.

"Why don't I sit in on this one?" Dan offered. "Just in case." She started to object but he held up his hands. "It's your first day back and it's a new drug. Let's go with prudence over pride, just this once."

His heart was pounding, being so direct with her—she with the perpetual chip on her shoulder anyway. But he saw her shoulders deflate—evidently seeing the wisdom in it. "Okay, let's scrub up," she said.

The patient was a middle aged white guy. He was in good shape, Dan noted, which was good, since extra weight always meant that a higher dose would be necessary.

"Am I going to wake up with a headache?" the man asked Clare.

"Did you taper off your coffee this past week?" she asked.

"Uh...no," he admitted.

"Then you're probably going to have a whopper when you wake up, but it's not going to be from the anesthetic."

"Hoo boy."

"Just relax and think good, caffeinated thoughts," Clare said, and put the induction mask over his nose and mouth. In moments, his breathing had slowed. Expertly, she monitored his heartbeat and blood pressure. She removed the induction mask and sat back. "How am I doing?"

"You're a pro," Dan smiled at her. It was good to have her back.

"So what else do I need to know about this stuff that the journals don't tell me?"

He shrugged. "Toxicity is less than Enflurane, so it's safer. Still, for a guy this size, you don't want to push 200 milligrams."

She nodded. Just then the man stirred and began to moan slightly.

"Here it comes," Dan said. "Like clockwork."

"Come here....dammit! Come...don't struggle," the man said, moving his head slightly.

"Is he deep enough?" Clare asked.

"He's fine. Just listen," Dan leaned forward, eager to hear the next thing the man would say.

"Hold your head like that....your eyes are....beautiful. No, don't be afraid. I want to say that I'm not going to hurt you...but it's not true. I *am* going to hurt you, and you *should* be afraid."

Clare looked at Dan, her eyes wide. Dan felt his throat go dry almost instantly. A chill ran down his spine.

"Yes, that's it. Scream," the man continued. "I *love* to hear you scream. Scream for me some more.....Oh, yeah. That's what makes me hot. Your eyes are nice."

"Should we call someone?" Clare asked.

"And tell them what? That a delirious guy is having drug-induced hallucinations?"

"This is no hallucination, Dan, and you know it. This is a memory."

Dan watched Clare carefully. He saw her jaw tighten; her fists, balled tight, began to shake.

"Okay, you've had enough time," the man mumbled. "It's time for Mr. Knife. Oh, don't be like that. It's just a knife. It will be over before you know it. It won't hurt...much. I'll do your eyes last...I promise."

Suddenly, Clare relaxed, wiped the sweat from her palms onto her scrubs. With calm resolve she picked up the induction mask. Over her shoulder she said, "Thanks for the help, Dan. I can take it from here."

a good day for redheads

By Patricia Abbott

It took me several foggy-headed seconds to realize the redhead standing in the doorway wasn't my ex. She was a dead ringer for Adeline circa 1985, though—same body type, same spiky hair, identical vague look in her eyes. Dressed in a shimmery blue dress, the girl couldn't have been more than twenty-five. I turned away quickly, but her eyes had already latched onto mine, zeroing in the same way Adeline's once had.

Was it the music that made me think of her? *Sweet Dreams*. Who was that redhead who sang it? I turned back to my third Bushmills and shook my head. A good day for redheads—always my weakness. I felt a tap on the shoulder, but smelled her perfume first. Spicy and sharp, a concoction for sirens.

"Hey, Mister." The scent rushed up my nose, and my pulse quickened. Damn, if I could help myself.

The bartender, hammering at some ice, looked up and frowned. I got the message—the redhead was trouble. I bore down on my drink.

"Mister," she said again. Her voice was throaty, irresistible.

A tug on my sleeve, and I turned without thinking—pretty much how I did everything after a few drinks. Up close, she was even younger. I straightened up a little. "Yeah?"

"Wonder if you'd take a look at my car?"

"I'm no mechanic, Miss." Her eyes looked silvery-green in the dim light, fox-like.

"Worked fine yesterday, but now it won't start."

"Kimmy, call Bud at the Sunoco!" the bartender said. "This guy's busy."

"Don't look busy," she said, catching my eye again. "You busy, Mister?"

The bartender sighed a sigh that said I couldn't handle Kimmy. It made me stand up a bit faster, straighten my back. Never could resist a siren call.

"Don't say I didn't warn you."

"Name's Doake if you don't see me again," I said, smiling weakly at the barkeep. I pushed through the door.

"Did you say Dope?" he shouted after me. The door slammed shut.

"Where's your car, honey?" I asked, blinking in the fierce light. A mosquito buzzed nearby and I slapped on my hat. Seemed to me mosquitoes will hang around all day waiting for a hairless head.

"Out at my house in Shelterville."

"You walked into town? Why not call a mechanic like the bartender said?"

"I just need a jump."

I'll give you a jump all right, I thought to myself. Truth be told, I was thinking of Adeline again—remembering those days when jumping didn't hurt my knees. But instead I drove Kimmy out to her place.

A lopsided house sat back in the trees, its steps a half-foot off the ground and the door flung open all wild-like. Someone had burned garbage not long ago and my nose stung with it.

"Can see why it won't start," I said, peering into the window of an old Escort. A guy heavier than me was slumped over the wheel and dashboard, dressed in a suit that didn't look like it came from Value City. "Ever seen him before?"

"Sure," she said. "Mayor Parker. Came out last night for a pick-me-up."

"Looks like he was disappointed." I opened the door and pried him loose. A hole bullseyed his middle. I looked around. "He walk out here? Lots of people walkin' in...Shelterville...huh?"

She narrowed her foxy eyes in contemplation. "Look, I gotta get to work, Mister. I got a day job at Safeway's. Can you get him outta there?"

"Well even if I do, Kimmy, I doubt you can just drive off to work. We got us a murder here." I noticed traces of blood on the gravel. "Looks like someone dragged Mayor Parker from elsewhere."

I began following the drops. The blood stopped just east of a large hole. I peered down. It was no natural hole. Someone had back-hoed it into existence—its sides were sloped, its base cavernous. At that bottom, a huge fellow sat on a stool. At least, I think there was a stool beneath his deep stratums of fat. He had the same red hair as Kimmy—maybe a tad more orange in it.

"Who's that?"

"That's my brother, Tiny," Kimmy said. Tiny turned up his face and grinned, showing me his wall-to-wall choppers. A couple or more were missing, but I'd bet it didn't slow him down much.

"What's he doing in that hole?"

"Iffin Tiny gets outta there, he does bad things," she told me. "Stays down there 'cept when I throw 'im that chain." She nodded toward a chain fastened to a huge metal anchor. The links in that chain would circle a bigger neck than Tiny's.

"You throw that chain down there last night?"

She nodded. "But it wasn't Tiny killed Mayor Parker. Tiny just tore up his car a little. Drove it into a ditch. Chased him around some. Had hisself some fun." Tiny roared his approval, and I stepped back from the hole.

"Tiny's pretty hungry now. Been waiting a long time for his dinner." She paused. "That's where you come in, Mister."

"Who killed the Mayor?" I asked, mesmerized by the chain of events despite my good sense.

"I did. I blew that hole clear through 'im."

"Why d'ya kill him, Kimmy?"

"'Cause I needed to get Tiny his dinner." I felt her hand at the small of my back, no more than a whisper of heft to it. "Seemed like a good way to get some'un out here. Been known to work before." She shoved, and I slid down into the hole like a Finn on skis.

"Let me get this straight," I shouted, once I picked myself up. "You murdered that obese mayor so you could put him behind the wheel of your car, come into town, tell me it wouldn't start, then drag me out here for Tiny's dinner?" Could this be her reasoning? "Why didn't you just feed Mayor Parker to Tiny?"

"Tiny's not overly partial to government handouts. Ain't that right, Tiny?"

Tiny roared, his mouth two inches from my ear.

the good samaritan

By Jami Reeves

I stopped my car in the middle of the street and checked the address again. The dilapidated cabin looked as if it would collapse at any second. The numbers on the mail box matched the address in the wallet. This had to be the place. I shook my head doubtfully, then pulled into the driveway.

The boards bowed and creaked as I carefully climbed the steps. A cold wind whipped across the porch, billowing my skirt around my legs. Wrapping my arms tightly around myself, I turned and looked over the yard. The large, ancient oaks gently waved their branches. Golden leaves shimmered in the daylight as they floated to the ground. The pastoral scene was reminiscent of grand Southern plantations, but for the nasty shack blemishing the surroundings. I sighed. I'd come to return the backpack, and the sooner I did the sooner I could shake off this deplorable place and get back to civilization.

At my knock, the door quickly opened. Big blue eyes looked up at me from a dainty, elvish face. The child looked angelic, except for the doll she carried. The hideous creation dangling from her tiny fingers looked like a horror film monster, its hairless scalp encrusted with nail heads. I grimaced at the sight, then quickly plastered on a bright smile. "Hi, there. Are your parents home?"

The girl said nothing, but continued staring up at me.

Clearing my throat, I said, "This backpack was left at my restaurant, and the wallet inside had this address. Um, is there anyone else here with you, honey? I really need to return this bag and get back."

Without a word, the girl walked away, leaving the door open. I leaned in and glanced around the living room. "Hello, is anyone here?" Seeing and hearing no one, I stepped inside.

The little girl huddled in the corner of the room, rocking back and forth, her thin arms wrapped around knobby knees. I knelt beside her. "Are you here alone?"

The girl nodded, her stringy, blonde hair bouncing up and down. She looked up and said, "You shouldn't be here. You have to leave."

"I can't leave you here alone. How long have you been by yourself? How long has it been since you had anything to eat?"

"You have to leave before he gets angry."

"Who?"

"Him."

My eyes followed the line of the short, bony finger, to the doll lying haphazardly on the floor. I looked back to the girl and saw genuine fear. "That's it. You can't stay here alone. You're coming with me."

I stood and grabbed the girl's hand. The front door slammed shut. I looked around. No one was in the room. I rushed to the door, but a stabbing pain in my foot stopped me short. The scary doll's hand was wrapped around a nail protruding from the top of my foot. She tried to kick it away. Blood spurted from the puncture when I pulled the nail out, throwing it and the doll across the room. The crimson liquid filled my Jimmy Choo.

The little girl curled into a fetal position on the floor, softly crying and sucking her thumb. I tried to lift the girl, but she struggled and cried out.

"We have to leave," I yelled.

The girl cried, "I can't leave. You have to go. Go now while you still can."

I clutched the girl tighter and limped closer to the door, closer to freedom. I felt the stab in my back just before my legs gave way. I reluctantly let go of the child to reach behind myself, finding a nail lodged in my spine. My legs now paralyzed, I pulled myself towards the door. A second stab to my spine, and my bowels released. My arms became lifeless with the third nail.

I now lay on the floor in a puddle of my own urine, helpless, unable to move. "Why?" I cried.

"I told you to go, but you wouldn't listen. He demands blood. He demands the sweet-tasting souls of good Samaritans."

"The backpack. It was a ruse?"

The girl nodded.

"But I was just trying to be a good person, to do the right thing. Why?"

"Only good souls sustain him. He won't let me leave. He keeps me to lure them in. I had hoped you could finally save me, but I knew you wouldn't."

"But how?"

"He is my demon," the girl said with a smile.

"Your demon?"

The angelic face contorted. Sky-blue eyes darkened to black. Features elongated, and sharp canines escaped her lips. "It seems I have lied. My pet merely incapacitates my prey for me. It is I who demand blood. I needed you to feel compassion for me. You just can't imagine how delicious it makes you taste."

The girl lunged on top of me. As teeth sank into my neck, I wondered how my life had come to this moment. Before I could grasp the answer, my life faded into nothingness.

a grace note,
fallen by the wayside....

By Cornelius Fortune

The Last Jazz Musician licked his lips for the third or fourth time, but it did little to help. The sound wasn't as clear as he remembered. The trumpet, a gold battered thing, hung limp at his side.

The cool autumn air touched his cheeks, and gave him a reason to raise the mouthpiece again, rust-colored from his own blood, back when it would flow easily, and his steps were assured, not dragging, ambling movements. He leaned against the tree with the swinging car tire that bumped his leg at intervals. It belonged to one of his daughters, but which one, he'd never know again, the deterioration of his flesh taking up residence in his mind. Nor did he actually care.

His family's blood nourished the dandelions and over-grown weeds of the front yard. It had fallen to rotting wood posts; bloated water-stained mail, thick and forgotten, a religious tract declaring everlasting life. The cherished car he'd never drive on the highway again, caked with dust and grime, with the midday sun striking the windshield at an angle that would have been uncomfortable to his eyes were they not so different now (everything was filtered through an oily grey and pink; like staring into rainbow puddles touched with gasoline).

He worried about nothing, thought of nothing. All that was left was the music.

Before, it was a simple life, more or less. He made a few critically-acclaimed records; one reviewer from a well-respected magazine called him, "the Last Jazz Musician," and the name stuck. What he had been before—his name, and family—that was gone, too. But some conversations lingered; the ones that counted the most, maybe; the conversations with his wife.

After dinner they'd sit on the porch and talk awhile. The kids were in bed. Time seemed to stretch out in those moments, and he appreciated the soft brush of her hands. She'd asked him about what he would do after the music. It was so dark they could barely see one another's faces.

"You're saying I can't do this forever? I disagree."

There was no offense in his voice at all.

"Not forever," she said. "No one has forever."

"This is what I'll always be, Melanie."

Even now, he cradled his trumpet and blew a few quiet notes, the dented Harmon mute, giving his tone an otherworldly distinction, a ghostly echo in the warm summer night.

"This will never change, not in my lifetime," he said, touching her knee with the trumpet's bell. "I go on a machine for life support, you be sure my horn's near me."

"And what will you do? Wake up from the dead?"

He caught his wife's smile in the dark, the way she accepted his eccentricities as if they were just another product of nature.

"Anything's possible," he said, sounding like a fool to his own ears. But music was his very salvation, the one religion he truly believed in.

This was a small town, population 15,000 and declining,

and the CDC's warnings weren't taken very seriously. That is, until people started getting sick. The old graves remained undisturbed, though the recently dead were another matter entirely.

Standing outside the house where his wife and children had died screaming, devoured by those mindless creatures who ate insatiably—mostly human meat, but sometimes the occasional house pet—he waited for his family to rise. He waited days—but they never did. Scattered as randomly as litter dragged across a lawn, the bodies slipped into decomposition; just as he slipped into depression, playing out scenarios in his head. Had he been there sooner, and not on the bandstand, earning the cash that would pay the month's mortgage. If not save them, he could have at least died with them.

There, with the remains of his dead family strewn about the yard, he removed his trumpet from its case and played in grief. He couldn't be sure if it was his scent or his questing, broken tones that brought the flesh eaters back to his home, but they came for him and he accepted his death, and the rending of flesh; he knew without a doubt that, like his family, he would not come back.

Then he rose up from that deep sleep, reached for his horn, and licked lips with the piece of sandpaper that used to be his tongue. The hunger for musical exploration, complex improvisations, hitting the perfect note that would narrate his story and interpret his once-pain, eased the hunger for flesh.

He worked at his craft for weeks.

And then he saw the angry people.

Some in cars, others on foot, armed with an assortment of items. He could not speak, and any attempt to communicate with them would be misinterpreted as hostile, but he could still play his horn. After all, music was a universal language, even music played by the undead.

So came the last performance of the Last Jazz Musician. He played furiously in hopes that they could hear his humanity (however altered) shine through in a mournful tune, a bluesy downbeat. As the music surged through his system, he had to be careful not to sway too much, lest his lifeless body fail him.

The Last Jazz Musician played on until a woman with hatred in her eyes (a woman clearly hurt by the same pain that had brought him to this very place), raised an axe, and separated his head from his body, a grace note dying bitterly in the wind.

As his thoughts faded to nothing at all, he realized he had finally hit the perfect note.

the grange

By John R. Mabry

Joe watched his father as he did every night. The man worked his land until sunset, and then, just as the last shards of daylight were fading, he would lean on his hoe and survey his fields. There was something about the sight of the old man in silhouette against the orange sky, supported by that old rusty hoe that lit a flame of comfort within him. It was a ritual that his father observed every day, without fail. Watching him was Joe's ritual. Seeing it meant that he could lie down for the night with a full and peaceful heart.

The next day was like every other—filled with back-breaking labor as they worked to eke a living out of this poisoned soil. Before the Illumination, as the locals called it, this had been the "Breadbasket of America." Then came the great flash of light, that had left half of the population of the little town nearby blind, and half again had died the next year from a mysterious sickness that the grownups called "radation."

As the sun tipped toward the fields, Joe froze. He was hauling a bucket of water out to his dad when the horsemen rode in. "The Grange," Joe breathed. Their faces were covered, but he knew who they were. They all lived in the town, and they were rich—as rich as anyone could be in this new world.

"You've been holding back on us, Cal," said their leader, stopping just short of the scarecrow Joe's father had made last year. Joe recognized Earl Beck despite the kerchief over his mouth. He always wore that same worn, straw hat.

"I ain't holdin' back nothing, Earl, and you know it," Joe heard his father say. He held his hand up toward Joe—a sign that Joe took to mean, "don't come no closer."

"You know the penalty for holdin' out," Cal said, spitting tobacco from high atop his horse.

Joe's father removed his hat and wiped his sweat off onto his sleeve. He replaced his hat and spoke slowly and deliberately. "I don't want no trouble, Cal. I believe in contributing to the common good, but we got nothing in reserve, here. Look at Joe, there," he pointed back at his son. "Does he look like he's eating well? He's skinny as a rail. And I give him the lion's share."

"Grange dues are two pounds of grain out of ten," Cal said.

"I tell you what, when I get *four* pounds, I'll give you two." Joe's dad leaned on his hoe. "You know the seasons are crazy. *You* been able to harvest yet?"

"We're not talking about my farm. I pay my dues," Earl said. "So does every man here," he gestured at the other riders. They nodded in agreement.

"What you gonna do, Earl? Take the dirt?"

"We're here for one of two things: grain or justice. Your choice."

"Earl, if you can find any grain on this farm, it's yours."

"Then I guess we'll have to settle for justice," Earl swung down from the saddle, and swift as a rabbit, he drew his knife and slashed at Joe's father's throat. Blood leaped into the air, black against the orange sky, and his father fell to the dirt as limp as a rag doll.

Earl swung back into his saddle and rode to where Joe was standing, eyes wide and hands shaking. "Two pounds out of ten," he repeated, and then, as if a flock of birds in formation, the Grange rode away towards the town.

Joe rushed to his father, tears streaming from his eyes. He fell upon the body, lifeless now, and already cooling. Joe bunched his father's shirt in his fists and pushed at his chest as he wailed.

In a few minutes, the wave of grief subsided. The world felt out of control, and Joe fell to the earth himself, seized by a feeling of vertigo. He rolled on the ground and wept until the silence and the coolness of the breeze tugged at his attention. It was almost time—the time he looked forward to every night. Tonight, of all nights, he needed their ritual.

He ran to the barn and pulled out a roll of gray, tough tape—a precious possession his father cherished and used sparingly. He had called it "Duck tape," but Joe did not know what a "duck" was.

He ran back to where his father's body lay. With a groan, he roused his father's lean frame and carried it over his shoulder to where the scarecrow stood. He ripped the scarecrow down easily, the weather-worn rope coming to pieces with a sharp tug. With great effort he heaved his father's body up into position on the crossed pieces of wood and taped them into place. He taped his father's head up, so that he surveyed the fields he had worked so hard. Finally, he taped the hoe to his father's fingers, just so, so that when he stood back, it looked like his father was leaning on it. It was the best that he could do.

Through his tears, Joe wandered back to the farmhouse. He turned to look at his father in silhouette against the red-streaked sky. He took a deep breath, and willed the little flame of comfort into life.

helen damnation

By Anthony Ambrogio

The Thinking Reed Carnival fire consumed the entire sideshow.

Blaise Passe-Gueule found himself on an apparently clothes-optional streetcar slowly spiraling southward, next stop Hades, along with his colleagues, including Squidgy the midget (naked as a jaybird, and much taller than Blaise remembered), Hirsute the Bearded Lady (face and entire body smooth as a nectarine), and his own dear wife, Ava Lee (more beautiful and nude than ever, though he distinctly remembered her blistering beside him in the earthly inferno that had sent them to this unearthly one).

"We're all naked lost souls here," someone whispered in his ear. Blaise turned to see a man wearing a toga and a conductor's cap—the only person in the entire car not baring it all. "All naked lost souls, retaining the best attributes of our earthly life. Look in this mirror." And Blaise was pleasantly surprised by the un-fire-damaged figure he cut in the afterlife.

The man addressed them all. "Hello, I'm Virgil, your tour guide on our descent. Fasten your seat belts; it's going to be a bumpy night."

They corkscrewed down the circles of hell, eventually coming to rest in front of the Paradise Lost Arms, an art-deco skyscraper with stylized-flame motif. "Last stop. Everybody out," Virgil sang.

Blaise asked the question on everybody's mind: "Are we in hell?"

"No, just purgatory. No need to abandon hope, all ye who enter here; check it at the door for pick-up later. Now: into the lobby, and I'll explain the rules."

They filed out and lined up, aware of their nakedness now, in the face of the smirking devils and minor demons of the hotel staff. Blaise and Ava Lee, side by side, clasped hands for mutual comfort and support.

"Okay," said Virgil, striding before them, like a general inspecting his troops, "if you successfully suffer for your sins here, you go to heaven. Everyone gets a room—*separate* rooms for everyone. You sit and burn for the requisite time. Then you pass on." He pointed a finger upward.

"How long?"

"Depends on the severity of your sins." Virgil activated the computer in his palm. "Hmm...the shortest duration is...500 years." Their faces fell. He looked up. "Hey, it's not so bad. Time'll fly by; you'll see."

"We've just been through a fire that lasted only a few minutes. The pain was unbearable! Can't we do anything to shorten our sentences?"

Virgil considered. "There's one thing. But it's a gamble. Choose two champions who'll be put to the Test. If they both succeed, you all pass on immediately. If not...well, hell isn't so bad this time of year—110 in the shade, if you can find any shade."

"Show us what to do."

Virgil led them to two adjoining doors: *Helen Damnation* on the left. *Hal Phyre N. Brimstone* on the right.

"Neither Helen nor Hal—dark angels, favored of Satan—has been, *ahem*, 'satisfied' for millennia. Satisfy them, and you're all free to go."

"What's the problem? Is she repulsive?"

"She's quite—'hot.' Just never found the member that could satisfy her."

"Is that all?" The carny boys exchanged smirks.

"Before you get too, uh, 'cocky,' observe!" Virgil warned.

The left door opened. Helen Damnation's latest suitor was dragged out, screaming and sobbing, genitals melted, pubic hair smoldering.

"I *said* she was hot."

"Is *he* 'hot' too?"

"No. He's 'sharp.'"

The right door opened, and Hal Phyre's most recent paramour was carried out, limp and moaning, blood gushing from a belly wound made by some cut from the *inside*.

"Want to reconsider?"

"No," said Blaise. "We'll try."

* * *

Helen's dark lair was illuminated by her own firelight. Reclining wantonly, legs splayed, on a raft of fire-retardant cushions, she was as attractive as any woman Blaise had ever seen, almost as beautiful as his own Ava Lee—save for the flames that periodically spewed from her vagina.

"What have we here?" Her voice was like honeyed magma. "Has the little boy come to douse my fire and quench my thirst? Is your hose sufficient, your loins girded in asbestos? Or are you one of those fools who believe they can pleasure me before I give them the third degree—in and out before Old Faithful spurts again?"

"They've all approached it wrong." Blaise counted the beats between the hot expulsions of her womb.

"Really?"

"You need the right kind of man."

"You? How do *you* expect to properly approach me?"

In answer, Blaise, having caught her rhythm, threw himself on all fours, put his mouth to her labia and commenced licking. When she exploded, he captured the tongue of fire in his mouth, expelled it in another breath, then continued his cunnilingus.

Initially startled, she soon caught *his* rhythm, quickened her pace, and finally climaxed in a volcanic burst of flames.

They lay together afterward, she quietly smoking, a satisfied smile upon her lips. "That was the best I ever had," she murmured. "The underworld moved. ...They *were* approaching it from the wrong direction. How did you manage—"

"I was a fire-breather with the circus."

She admired the elegance of the solution. "So I did need the right kind of man!"

"After this, I think anyone will do." Blaise rubbed her clitoris, which responded with a weak shower of sparks. "See? From now on, all your fire will be internal."

"Blaise Passe-Gueule, you wonderful man. For freeing me from this thrall, you deserve swift passage to heaven—but you've one more hurdle to overcome. And your powers are useless against it. Hal Phyre's nether weapon can split a woman's privates or a man's anus like a knife!"

"I know. My wife is handling him."

"She'll be sliced in two—"

"She'll take the same approach as I."

"But how can oral sex save her?—"

"*She* was a sword swallower with the circus."

the honeymoon

By Matthew Wilson

The end of the road was only the start of the problems.

Richard sighed and re-checked his map. He had to be close to it. He had to admit that the desert did not make for a good honeymoon, but then he had never intended to get married in the first place, let alone see the holiday through to the end.

She had tricked him, as simple as that, by simply getting pregnant. He didn't believe her when she said she had lost the pills. It was just one weekend when she had not protected herself, but apparently it had been enough before her quick dash to the chemist's first thing Monday morning.

She had been a poor woman when he met her, so maybe she was chasing some security. Maybe she had planned it all along, to trap him, but now he was a prisoner no longer. He had a plan, a chance of escape. The cave was just up ahead. And only he would walk out of there alive.

Life was nine-tenths planning to get what you want. And one-tenth self-concern. Consideration to other human beings must be discarded, and this one single tenth must be as potent as the sun's rays. Strong, almost rabid. There could be no turning back now.

Friends had told him that she was a gold digger, only after

his money, but he knew she was too dumb for that. She was stupid for thinking she could pull this off. He had planned the vacation: the accident inside the cave would be no problem.

She seemed to snap awake from her romance paperback when she felt the car rock once, and stop. "Are we here?" "We sure are, babe." He killed the engine and saw her glow when he called her that: as if it were a tag of his affection for her, as if she were a woman someone could actually care about. He had worked hard for his money: a separation would suck a great deal of it from his bank account. If he hadn't married her then she would have always been there in the background taking her maintenance checks.

Another mouth to feed. But now that she had a ring on her finger, she was relaxed enough to go along on the honeymoon: it was what normal husbands and wives did. Time to unwind and have some fun, before she expected him to support herself and her baby.

The money was his. His!

Such a silly creature: good-looking, though, as most silly things were. He knew she had the power to wind a lesser man around her finger: which had been one of her initial attractions, but now he was free from her spell—free from everything about her.

She squinted as, invited, she got out of the car, covered her eyes with the heel of her hand against the glare of the sun, and watched. The hole in the side of the cliff looked like a waiting mouth that would swallow them whole.

"Yeah, it will be good to get you off that phone you've had to your ear all morning and get some experience of the world," Richard smiled, hating her more then he had ever hated another creature.

Becky smiled back. She wondered if the latest man she had wound round her finger was waiting in the dark of the cave, a heavy rock in his hands to bring down on her husband's head as they had planned.

Richard had taught her to be a planner.

"I have friends beside you," she teased, and held his hand to keep her balance as they went off-road, across the broken bits of cactus at their feet, hearing carrion birds screaming in the cloudless skies.

Becky squeezed his fingers, "Today will be better for both of us. You'll see," she said.

Richard agreed.

Together they headed toward the cave.

house hunting

By Sara Courtney

As you can see, this lovely home is just waiting for a nice couple like you! It just needs a bit of paint! The style back then was a bit odd, you know they must've thought red splotches on the wall was like modern art. Step right this way, don't be shy and don't worry about the chalk outline. There was a bit of a row with the last couple that lived here—actually, newlyweds, like yourselves—and as you can see it didn't end well. But don't let that deter you. Oh sure, there are always stories, "McCormick House is haunted!" goes everyone, and my friends all make fun of me, "You'll never sell that place!", but I can *see* the potential. And I can tell by the wide-eyed look on your faces that you can see it too! It just needs a nice couple like you! Follow me into the kitchen. Envision a beautiful breakfast nook over there, with the light coming in through the windows if they weren't all boarded up. Such a spacious kitchen! The layout is excellent for entertaining. This is a vintage refrigerator and it has quite a bit of storage space, as you can see from the second chalk outline. Yes, there is *lots* you can do in this kitchen! And you *did* ask to see a large home for under two-hundred thousand. Well, in a neighborhood like this, that is a *steal*! Practically *giving* the house away! Such a shame. Ah, but here, come over to the back door and take a look at the backyard. Look at the size of it! It is a good two acres and all the blackberry bushes you ever wanted! Now, a nice young couple like yourselves only need a little bit of grass, you don't have any kids yet—although by the looks of you one is coming soon—but look here, you don't need to worry about mowing all the time. And for you, miss, there is a beautiful rose patch over there by those tombstones. Yes, a bit unusual, the house is so old and you know how people back then had their quirks. Well, the McCormicks always insisted on burying their dead on their own land. They were a big family in town, too. The great grandfather was a mayor, though he died in prison but that was on account of town politics which is always corrupt. And the grandmother ran a knitting group of some kind which lots of women in town joined—why, she ran it right out of the living room here. What a piece of history you could be a part of! Legend has it, it was so successful that men frequented it all the time, so I guess they were exciting knitters—if there is such a thing. Let's go upstairs to see the bedrooms. No—that's not the way upstairs, that's the front door! And you will find the door is locked. Well, there's no use tugging at the thing, you're liable to break it! By the way, did I tell you that I'm a McCormick, too? I inherited the house—moved in with my wife right after we got married. She's out back by the rose bushes, maybe you saw her. Now come upstairs. I insist. It's funny thing how people always want to leave. Can't they ever figure out there is no leaving? But I tell you one thing the blackberries sure are sweet. Wait till you try 'em.

how it ended for jasper malyhe

By Morgen Knight

The reservations were going to be wasted, but there was no helping that. It was a good thing he hadn't mentioned them to Kitty. She would be at home right now, dolling up, excited to have a break from the boxed dinners and shoe-string meal plans.

Jasper dragged himself down the busy city street. His hand loosened his tie with a series of merciless yanks, hating the way the tie felt. Too tight. Everything felt too tight, constricting. One hand was in his pocket, fingering the loose change there. He had crumpled up his résumé while he was still inside Danworth and Mitchell's lobby; he hadn't bothered to throw it away. Let it sit on the buffed tile floor. The janitor would see to it; that man had a job.

He moved forward with his head down, not really thinking or hearing or caring. This had been his millionth interview. Ever since the Great Recession, it seemed like all of his degrees weren't worth the paper they were printed on. He hated the hopeful gleam in Kitty's eyes every time he went out. The pressure of that hope made it hard for him to breathe. And day after day, when he returned with this beaten expression, that hope briefly winked out, and looking in her eyes was like looking into a dark room. What he hated the most was when that gleam vanished, when he felt like less than a man.

"Flee! Flee before the rising terror. Hear this final call and turn your heart from evil!" a man was crying out.

Jasper looked for the voice, realizing that he had been hearing the man's crazy words for more than a minute. Jasper stopped; he stood in the middle of the sidewalk while people instinctively routed around him. Everyone was bundled in heavy coats and scarves. Jasper barely felt the winter cold.

"It is the end!" the man yelled out. "Death is no longer waiting at the door. He's letting Himself in!" The man was dirty. His hair was stringy and slick with grease. His coat had patches on it, holes. His brown beard had thick bands of white. When the man began to belt out his warnings, Jasper saw his gums and the remains of stained teeth. The man had the intensity of madness, and Jasper couldn't help but think how easy his life must be. Stress free. Grab a street corner and yell at the world. How easy it would be to end this life and start that one.

Jasper slowly continued forward. Dim sunlight reflected off the windshields of all the passing vehicles. Tall art-deco buildings gave the street a claustrophobic feel, and a sense of how small he really was.

"And the Earth will shake, the monuments made by men will crumble. From Hell a thousand beasts will emerge. And for the few, God will send his angels. Call out now. REPENT!" the man said. As Jasper passed, the man looked at him; their eyes met. "Do you know the cost of death?" Fog plumed from his dry mouth.

Jasper moved on like you're supposed to. Never stand near the crazy or the wild. Like animals, they may bite.

He stopped next to a magazine kiosk. "Economic Collapse" ran across the *Conception Gazette*'s front page.

"Despair growing" was in smaller letters. "News flash," he said to himself. He looked at the busy street and the rising tails of exhaust, feeling what the paper had named. Each step closer to home added pounds to the weight on his back. He didn't think they could hold onto their home. They had tapped out what credit they had; borrowed from family, and then from friends. There wasn't a drop left to squeeze out. All of their insurance policies were going to lapse. Hopefully the kids wouldn't get sick. And if anything happened to him, they'd be on their own. Except for the life insurance, and that would lapse in three weeks.

"Do you know the cost of death?"

Jasper didn't, but he knew that he could do more for his family dead than alive. He had a million-dollar policy. No more food donations or clothes charities. No going without a phone or lights for a month while necessities were juggled. No more looks of disappointment or that eerie silence. *He could do it*, he told himself. It would be quick. It would be more than he had done for his family in over a year.

Jasper walked to the street, tottering on the curb. One quick step was all it would take. He saw a city bus coming. Something with that much mass had to be fatal, and quickly. Was he desperate enough to really do it? Tending forward, he thought that—

The ground violently shook. It lasted for over three minutes. Cars crashed. Glass from broken windows showered the street. Chunks of concrete and stone fell. People were screaming. Jasper had fallen between two stopped cars. His head took a hard blow. When he stood, blood was running from a cut in his brow, down his face.

"Oh, god," he said.

The street was destroyed. Water was shooting up, fissures ran through the crumbled street, cars were half in sinkholes, some were gone. Smoke from fires stood up like pillars, lifting to the turbulent sky above. Jasper watched the clouds begin to spin, creating a dark vortex. Purple lightning jumped within the clouds.

"It's here, it's here!" the madman shouted, delighted. He fell to his knees on the roof of a car and opened his arms to the sky.

Jasper watched in horror as two giant hands tore the vortex wider, and winged creatures descended in hordes on the city. "Oh, god." And from below, out of the cracks, began to emerge the clawed reach of unspeakable beasts.

iDrone

by Sara Courtney

By the age of eight he had his own iPhone, iPad, two computers, and all the programs and games his heart desired. It kept him busy. His whole childhood played out in forests online, in jungles he navigated with the click of a mouse. He hacked into his first bank by the age of twelve. He transferred fifteen dollars from his geography teacher's bank account to the librarian's. Nobody ever knew. It was a small town. They'd never seen a genius before. And technology had hardly touched the place. Sure, everybody was online and a couple of eccentric writers and competitive moms had blogs, but still, people talked. When someone had a birthday, folks didn't just "like" it, they came out and celebrated.

He got his first drone at the age of fifteen. It was sleek and light-weight, only the size of his hand. The instructions were plain: "Users will find comfort in their ability to monitor their private property from trespassers. Caution must be exercised. Not a tracker."

He had a blast sending the drone to find his dog whenever he escaped. He was so adept at finding the mutt that for a while his mom was convinced he was psychic. He flew his drone over a spot in the forest he knew deer walked. He'd leave a ball of cheese and record them discovering it with delight.

For all his proficiency with the digital world, he couldn't figure out how to exist in the real one. He had no friends and no hobbies outside of spying on the dog with his drone.

He did dream of having a girlfriend. As long as he could remember, he liked Mary Walker. They'd been in school together since the 2nd grade. She was always so nice to him. Their lockers were near each other's and she always said hello. He didn't know how to say hello back.

When he hacked into her email he discovered she sub-scribed to a website called "Daily Inspiration." Their emails were clichéd. "Learn to love yourself and true happiness will follow." He wondered why she needed it.

When senior year came to a close, she asked him to sign her yearbook. She signed his with a smiley face. "Isn't it funny how our lockers were always right next to each others? I hope we see more of each other over the summer! Take care and remember—keep smiling. Mary." He wrote, "Happiness will follow."

He upgraded to an iDrone shortly before graduation. It had infrared cameras and a longer battery. He would send it out to check up on the dog. Then he'd fly it over to look at the deer, which always made him happy. Soon he found the iDrone flying over Mary's car as she drove home at night, and then hovering outside her bedroom window as she changed and brushed her teeth.

When prom came he watched from the sky. She danced with Thomas Wheeler, a football player. She looked happy twirling around the dance floor in her pink chiffon. He played the recording over and over. He wanted to learn how to dance.

He had made some changes to the iDrone. Minor ones. He installed a high-power laser to the front of it. When he had a bad day he would find nice cars and shoot the tires flat. Just a small slice and only a little bit of smoke, but the tire would quickly *hssssss* and he'd start to feel better. On the way home from prom, Thomas Wheeler got a flat tire. Mary's dad came and picked them up.

Then it was the night before graduation. He watched from the dark sky. The infrared picked up their two bodies in her bedroom. He felt the anger and humiliation and loss burn inside him. He would never learn to dance.

He set the laser on max, lowered his iDrone to her window, and it burned a clean slice through her wall, through their necks and there was no more movement picked up by the infrared.

It's a small town and everybody came to the funeral. They took pictures with their phones of the beautiful flowers and posted them online to a website dedicated in her memory.

After everybody left, he went. From the sky he lowered his drone and set it once more to max.

Weeks later the caretaker noticed the unusual grave of Mary Walker. Along with the dates of her life and death, it read:

Mary Walker
Daughter, Sister, Friend

And below that, in a curious scrawl:

Happiness Will Follow

It was almost as if someone had written it in stone.

in the night

By Nick Medina

Mark McNally knew which floorboards to avoid. He tip-toed over them like a cat doing ballet so as not to wake Tricia or the kids—Jonathan in his racecar bed and Sasha in her crib.

The three were everything Mark had ever wanted. She was beautiful; he was average. The kids were innocent; he wasn't. They could sleep; he couldn't.

So, in a chair by the bedroom window, he watched Tricia sleep. The bed sheet clung to her curves. Her right arm stretched across the empty half of the mattress as though searching for someone to hold.

Mark slowed his breathing to match hers. Together, their chests heaved in perfect unison. It made Mark feel as though things were right between them, as though they were one. When she eventually rolled over and nuzzled her face deeper into the pillow, Mark noticed that she still wore her wedding ring. He still wore his, too, though it had lost most of its meaning long ago.

Mark watched Tricia for over an hour. Sometimes he wanted to touch her. Sometimes he wanted to kiss her and whisper in her ear. But those things, he knew, would only garner rejection.

The pillow, though, next to Tricia's—empty and invit-ing—called to him. If only he could lie down next to her. They could share a bed and a blanket and their lives could be as one. They could tend to the kids in the morning and make dinner at night. But if he lay down, she would wake. And then all hell would break loose. Maybe worse.

I should go, he thought. *I should just make myself comfortable on the couch*. His want, however, wouldn't let him leave. He moved his nose close to her skin and inhaled deeply. The scented lotion she used intensified his ache. Inhaling again, he let his innermost being absorb her intrin-sic nature off the air. If he couldn't be inside of her, then she would be inside of him. As insubstantial as it seemed, he rel-ished her sweet taste until the ache inside gave way to accept-ance, whereupon he finally felt able to satiate himself in other ways.

Mark padded down the hallway, bypassing the children's rooms in pursuit of the kitchen, where crumbs—which he brushed into the sink—dotted the countertops. A greasy pot sat on the stove. Dirty dishes needed to be washed. Mark snagged the sponge to make Tricia's job easier, but then reconsidered and opened the refrigerator instead, helping himself to leftovers he thought might fulfill him since he couldn't have what he truly craved.

His stomach full and his mind off Tricia, Mark slipped inside Jonathan's room. The walls, covered with crayon drawings, always made him smile. He eyed a sketch that hadn't been there the day before. Jonathan had drawn him-self just as tall as Tricia while depicting Sasha as a bundle between their feet. Jonathan's caricature was smiling. Tricia's was not. One key member of the family was missing.

Sighing, Mark knelt next to the racecar bed to straighten Jonathan's twisted pajama pants. Jonathan's eyelids fluttered in response, and then he moaned. Mark recoiled. The moaning wasn't unusual. Jonathan had been doing that a lot lately. Mark just couldn't help but wonder if the moans were brought on by nightmares involving him. Fearing that his presence might scar the boy, Mark kissed Jonathan's cheek and crossed the hall.

Sasha was standing in her crib when Mark entered her room. She smiled at him and let out a laugh that sounded like a song.

Nearly melting inside, Mark scooped Sasha up in his arms.

"How's my girl?" Mark said.

Sasha responded with another giggle while Mark pressed his nose against the fuzzy top of her down-covered head. She smelled different than Tricia. Different, though no less lovely.

"You're wet," he said, feeling the heft in her diaper. She smiled some more and pointed one of her chubby digits at the dimple in his chin. "Let's get you changed."

Mark swapped the diaper for a clean one and covered Sasha with powder, making her smell all the more innocent and sweet, before settling into the rocking chair that would lull Sasha into the land of sandmen and wooly sheep, where he stayed until the glow from the sun crept up on the horizon.

Returning to the living room, Mark dropped onto the couch, whereupon his eyes landed on the framed photograph atop the coffee table. The frame was the same as it had been for years, but the picture it held was different; Tricia must have swapped it during the day. Like Jonathan's drawing, it was one member short of a complete family.

Maybe it's Tricia's way of dealing with the change, Mark thought. *Maybe it's her way of coping.*

He picked up the frame and squinted at the snapshot, trying to determine when and where it had been taken, trying to imagine where he would have been posed. Perhaps he would have had Jonathan on his lap with his arm around Tricia while she cradled Sasha in her arms.

Just as he perfected the unlikely image in his mind, the squawk-like screech of Tricia's alarm clock echoed down the hall, nearly making Mark drop the frame. Trembling, he put it in its proper place and stood. With his right hand exploring his pocket in search of the key he kept there, he headed for the door, thinking about the photo of the family—the mother and her children—the entire time.

Tricia Channing, recently widowed, would never think of Mark the way he thought of her. She would merely go on regarding him as Mr. McNally, the landlord downstairs.

Disheartened, Mark noiselessly locked Tricia's apartment on his way down to his own, where he'd struggle to endure the lonesome life thrust upon him when his wife left. Maybe one day he'd tell Tricia how he felt about her. Maybe when she was awake.

the intern

By Sara Courtney

On Tuesdays she picked up files from legal and ran them to the investor's assistants. Then she made copies of petty cash receipts for the staff; she wondered how $200 worth of sushi and a meeting at a club called "Bouncing Bette's" could be written off as a business expense. In the later afternoon she took everyone's coffee orders. Although there was one other intern besides herself, a pretty, unnaturally thin, perpetually manicured college senior named Cameron Danner, the intern always did this on her own. She noticed all the investors drank black coffee. A few of the older gentlemen went for herbal tea. But the assistants had the most complicated orders. Theirs was something with soy; extra shots; a few squirts of different flavors. She discovered early in her internship that it was dangerous to screw up someone's food or coffee order. Losing millions in a client's life savings was forgivable, but messing with someone's appetite was not.

It was Tuesday evening during the last week of her internship at Chosen Venture Capitalists and she had just been given a strange To Do list by the CEO Luce Ferrano. On posh paper with "LF" monogrammed on top were the words: "Black garbage bags. Shovel. Rope. Drill." As she looked it over, Cameron sauntered over. "What's that?" She smiled sweetly. Cameron's uncle was the Chief Operating Officer. She was connected and no doubt getting hired. *Another ivy league asshole,* thought the intern. They couldn't be more different. The intern went to Lynntown Community College. But she was persistent—determined to get ahead. She worked part-time as a courier and began dropping her résumé in mailboxes. Eventually she got an interview for one of the most elite internships in her field. She practiced her interviewing skills and knocked it out of the park. (She found out later that she only got it because an executive's nephew declined so he could go to Europe. No matter. Eventually she got it.)

"I'm running an errand for Mr. Ferrano," the intern said. She saw a brief flash of concern on Cameron's face before she snatched the list out of her hands and giggled.

"Doing some landscaping?!" Cameron teased.

The intern's face turned bright red. "Give it back!"

Cameron pulled the list out of reach and flashed a nasty smile. "I'm being offered a position. Invited to sign a contract tonight. But you have fun...weeding!"

"I will," she said stupidly.

Later while finishing at the hardware store her phone rang. It was Cameron. "Hello?" She waited. A prank. She listened closely and thought she heard quiet breathing. Suddenly she heard a cough—like Cameron's, but she sounded sick, as if she was coughing up something. *She's probably bulimic, sheesh,* she thought. *This is a butt dial.*

Then a garbled mumble: "Geh...elp."

The intern rolled her eyes. "By the way I have a job offer too." (It was true. Her uncle offered her a summer job working at his used furniture store.) "So don't get high and mighty—" At that the phone disconnected. She looked at her watch. It was approaching 9:30. By the time she dropped off Mr. Ferrano's gardening tools, it would be ten.

When she arrived, his door was closed but the light was peeking out. She knocked.

"Come in."

Sweaty, exhausted, her hair in her eyes, she lugged the bags into his office.

"Where would you like these, Mr. Ferrano?"

He smiled at her. "You've impressed me these past few months."

Silence filled the room.

"I have?"

"Yes. You have a bright future with us."

"I—I'd do anything to work here."

"That's good to know. As you know, we only hire one intern a year. You and Miss Danner worked very hard. But there was one more test. Miss Danner failed. I wonder if you will pass?"

"What is it?"

He smiled and walked to a large mahogany door—a closet—and opened it. Inside, tied with rope to a plush office chair that matched his furniture—was Cameron. Blood covered the left side of her face, her mouth was duct-taped, her eyes swollen with snot dripping from her nose. She was in a daze.

"I was completely out of rope—I hate that," Mr. Ferrano said cheerfully, retrieving the rope from the bag and tying it around Cameron's feet and torso. She could barely wriggle from the chair. Suddenly she became alert and at once was terrified. She looked at the intern and tears began to form. The intern looked from Cameron to Mr. Ferrano. "What is going on here?"

"We only hire one. Miss Danner did not pass our final test. For all her superiority—" (at this an ugly sneer curled at his lips) "—she couldn't bring herself to do it. So I am offering you a full time position, salary starting at $150—that's grand—plenty of room for growth. My assistant drew up your contract. Of course this is contingent on passing the last test." The intern looked at him and Cameron's terrified face and, slowly, understood.

"Do you have the drill?" The intern looked down at her bag. She thought about Cameron's life. She thought about her own. She thought about the economy and the unemployment and how hard she worked and how she was always watching people pass her because of their connections while she worked twice as hard as them.

"The drill. To her eyes."

The intern looked at Cameron. The duct tape came loose from all the tears and snot. "Get help! My God, he is crazy! He tried to get me to do this to you and I told him he was insane! Call my father!"

The intern picked up the drill. "Thank you for this opportunity, Mr. Ferrano." He smiled at her.

She brought the drill to Cameron's eyes. "I made it," she said proudly, though she didn't think Cameron heard over the drilling. When she finished, the intern smiled at her boss. "Where do I sign?"

intern shift

By Kate Gladstone

From: Justin Hirschman
To: TravelStudent Vacation Internships
Date: December 12
Subject: Reapplication
Enclosed please find my reapplication for the rainforest internship.

From: Bob Hirschman—Bob's Pre-Owned Vehicles
To: Arlene Capriolo, TSVI Coordinator
Date: December 12
Subject: Justin's reapplication
Thanks for reconsidering my son's application. As we discussed, my $10,000 donation to TSVI will be mailed on Justin's acceptance, followed by $15,000 when he completes the program.

From: Arlene Capriolo, TSVI Intern Coordinator
To: Justin Hirschman
Cc: Bob Hirschman—Bob's Pre-Owned Vehicles
Date: January 6
Subject: Congratulations!

Dear Justin:

Welcome to TSVI's Brazilian Rainforest Archeology Team! Please read the attached information. Note that internship begins with six weeks of training at our Miami campus.

Reminder: in the event of unsatisfactory performance, interns may be sent home at any time. Fees are *not* refunded.

TSVI looks forward to your success.

Arlene Capriolo—TSVI Coordinator

From: Frank Olensky, Field Team Director
To: Arlene Capriolo, TSVI Coordinator
Date: March 29
Subject: Justin Hirschman

Training passed this creep? He brags about skipping sessions. (Isn't that an automatic flunk?) He spends his day reading porno comics, blogging (don't interns leave their electronics in Miami?), hitting on local women (who laugh), and trying to bribe the local shaman, Wqihwe (who laughs harder), to make Justin a shaman.

Wqihwe laughs because Justin (having skipped language labs) attempts bribery by gesture.

He wasn't laughing today, though. Wqihwe's favorite wife caught Justin dropping Rohypnols into her drinking gourd. (She claims she destroyed them—I suspect they're in Wqihwe's medical kit.)

So the shaman's coming to give Justin a *wu'heo-yipqwue.* (Literally, that means "head-straightening." Nobody offers details beyond "It is what shamans do to useless youths."

At least the fact that Justin and Wqihwe have no shared language lets me come as interpreter: ordinarily, these ceremonies are private. So I'll wear my videocam transmitter.

From: Frank Olensky, Field Team
To: Arlene Capriolo, TSVI Coordinator
Date: March 30
Subject: Ceremony

I apologize for not sending video. Wqihwe had us disable all smartphones—then found my transmitter: "That, too."

Sure, I had another. He didn't seem to spot that—but it failed the instant he spotted the first bug. The next e-mail provides my notes.

The Hirschinator's Blog, March 31

After his videocam stunt, old Wiki-woohoo-whatever speechified—Frank translated—about how this ceremony brings power with the next full moon.

That's the night I fly home. Wiki-woohoo should sell used cars.

Anyway: W. made us go into my tent. There, he spooned out a bowlful of green powder and lit it. (Yup—shamans use cigarette lighters. At least, W. does.) He made me inhale (tasted like wet fur), then asked through Frank:

"What do you want to be if you grow up?"

The smoke made it hard to think of an answer (or anything else). I heard myself say: "Good-looking ... unique ... famous." W. claimed that'll happen if I change my ways. Three cheers for social control by priestcraft.

I'll be a good little intern. It's that, or fly home early so Dad screams I wasted his money again.

[TSVI Field Team Log of Frank Olensky:
Excerpt from translated transcript of ceremony]
Wqihwe: The next full moon brings magic.
Justin: Whatever. What kind of magic?
Wqihwe: That depends on how others see you. If someone calls you handsome, you may blaze like the sun. Swift—you

may fly like a condor, run like a jaguar. Strong—you may receive the strength of a great mountain or tree. If you are praised for some great deed—you may become a winged sky-man with a flaming machete, such as the missionaries talk about.

The Hirschinator's Blog, March 31
 So when I don't get superpowers, can I sue? Wiki-woo did act as TSVI's agent ...
 Then W. claimed it'd help if I trimmed my hair and mended my jeans.
 THANKS, Mister Etiquette. Know what jeans cost pre-ripped?!
  Fortunately, I'd seen W. sneaking peeks at my Collected Works of R. Crumb.
 So, sure, I agreed to work and do laundry—then did a repentance act: "Let me make you a gift: these books I shouldn't read instead of working.
 "While I learn to manage responsibility, how about postponing the grooming lecture till you're sure I'm handling the big stuff?" Frank translated that, but doubted W. made bargains. He jumped when the shaman stated my appearance wouldn't hurt anyone but myself.

From: Arlene Capriolo, TSVI Intern Coordinator
To: Bob Hirschman—Bob's Pre-Owned Vehicles
Date: April 8
Subject: Justin Hirschman
Magic? Rainforest psychotherapy? Frank says Justin has become a valued intern!
 (Note: TSVI accepts PayPal.)

The Hirschinator's Blog, May 3
Why call this blogging? Blogs have readers. Dad's made

me set mine to invite-only—and withhold invitations "till this blows over."

The good part of the flight home: sitting behind two hot chicks. Both ignored me, though: chit-chattering away in that cute British accent that rhymes "were" with "hear."

As we disembarked and I tried to spot Dad, one of the chicks—the blonde—spotted me. She pointed, giggling. She told her friend what she thought I looked like.

My balance altered. My sneakers slipped off my...Hooves?

I heard a shriek: Dad. The blonde raised her camera as my skin sprouted fur.

Hooves, fur... Was I a satyr? (That could be fun...) No: four legs.

Unicorn? Pegasus? No.

The blonde's camera lens reflected a hornless, wingless form.

A deer—hornless in more ways than one: I was not a stag.

Dad's still trying to get YouTube to pull her clip.

Even if he does, I'm stuck home one night a month.

Out of the millions of insults in the English language, why did she have to pick the one that exactly matched her pronunciation of "were-doe"?

leaves falling into fire

By Gregory M. Thompson

I ran.

That's all I could do. The leaves covered my house in minutes. By the time I realized what was happening, my only escape was the front door. And I barely made it outside before the leaves connected to each other like puzzle pieces and sealed off the house altogether.

Ten maple trees stood firm and tall in all areas of my yard. Why the original builders of the home decided on so many trees in a medium-sized yard was beyond me. No way they could have predicted tonight, but still...

I bent over, catching my breath. A pause in the leaf bombardment allowed me to figure out a plan.

The ground had no leaves. Each of the leaves, so far, had managed to attach itself to one of two places: the house, or the surrounding fence around my lot. On the fence, the leaves towered higher than my head, so "making like a tree and leafing" was out. *Leafing*. The brain acted funny sometimes, but leafing was pretty funny.

A tree on the right side released a few floating leaves. Was it starting again?

Couldn't go back into the house. Unfortunate, because my house phone *and* my cell phone were inside.

The neighbors.

I strolled as close to the fence as I dared. When I approached, the wall of leaves bowed towards me as if someone was pushing their hands from the other side. I picked up a hefty rock and hurled it at my neighbor's house, aiming at a second-floor window. The rock missed to the right a little, but still thudded loudly. Should be enough to wake Bill, Harriet, or the teenager whose name eludes me.

More leaves started to fall from other trees: slowly, calculatingly Gravity was the only thing saving me at the moment. The only trajectory for the leaves was down. Thank you, Newton.

I returned my gaze to my neighbor's house. No lights came on.

I slapped my forehead. They were on vacation in Florida, visiting Bill's mother. I remembered now: he had asked me to bring in the mail and newspaper.

A slight wind arose. It brushed my face with such delicate care, I almost didn't notice it.

The wind pushed around the leaves as they fell, twirling them and changing their direction. This was not good. I sprinted to a more open area of the yard, putting myself an equal distance between two trees.

I jammed my hands in my pockets, just in case I had unconsciously placed my cell phone in my jeans. I hadn't. But I did pull out a book of matches with the SHELL company logo stamped on the flap. Three weeks ago I quit smoking but kept the matches on me for comfort: much as someone finds comfort in their favorite book or in sitting in a comfortable chair or eating a familiar meal.

Leaves gathered around my feet, leap-frogging over each other to climb my tennis shoes. I stepped away. *He had asked me to bring in the mail and newspaper.* Newspaper!

I dashed to the porch, bounding up the stairs. I hadn't gotten the Saturday paper off the porch yet, and it lay face up: as if the masthead were saying, *Go ahead and use me; I'll sacrifice myself for you.*

When I picked it up, leaves from the porch railing reached out like ropes and looped themselves around my calves. I panicked and tried to step backwards, but I tumbled down the stairs. My head slammed against the pavement, an immediate throb rushing through my head. Stars appeared before me.

The tightness around my calves continued. My feet started to go numb.

I leaned up, extremely woozy. I closed my eyes and fumbled to open the matchbook. I ripped out a thin match, felt for the strike, and placed the match head on the friction strip. Pain entered my calf now, like a string being pulled tighter and tighter, willing itself to break skin and cut off my lower legs.

I opened my eyes, still dizzy, but feeling manageable. I struck the match and immediately held it near the leaves. They recoiled with ferocity and zipped back against the porch railing. I quickly backed up, ignoring the pain in my head and calves, and removed the first section of the paper.

Glancing around, the leaves almost entirely carpeted the grass. Soon, there would be no more grass. Only leaves. Deadly leaves.

The match lit and I held it to the newspaper, which caught and burned. The flame raced from the corner, threatening to engulf all of Section A and to disappear if I didn't add to it. I found two sticks near me and placed them carefully on top of the fire, then added more paper.

Suddenly, a thick throng of leaves sailed towards me. And the wind picked up. The flame flickered, almost extinguishing, but I cupped my hands around it before it could. The number of leaves intensified. They surrounded the paper, one or two landing directly in the flame kamikaze-style.

Crackles lifted up into my ears and I watched the leaves die.

And put out the fire.

I tried to strike another match, but more leaves than I had ever seen rained down on my arms, pushing them to the ground like fifty-pound weights. More leaves landed on my chest. My stomach, my thighs, my calves again, and my feet.

Trapped.

My face still remained free. How do leaves kill?

As leaves crawled in their own little way up my neck and chin, I knew. *Suffocation.*

And I let them win.

legion
oil on canvas, unsigned

By Keith Deininger

From the safety of the cold art gallery, the woman watched as the general raised his nail-spiked staff and brought it down to signal the charge, pointing it forward like a spear. The men let out a whoop and the world became a roaring blur of dust and shouting as their horses charged across the plain.

As they emerged from the fog of orange grit, the men could see their adversaries more clearly: painted faces of blood-red tears coming out of their wild eyes and running down their purple-tinted cheeks, and smeared pictographs on their chests and arms of dancing fiends and fish and the suns of other worlds. Horns cried out, the death knell of instruments made from bone, and the men reared up on their horses and began to pull back in confusion. And the legion came through the smoke.

They carried spears with ends like pipe organs, and blow-guns made from bone, and their purple skin was glistening and greasy like creatures from the ocean's depths, and they were beating their shields of shimmering reptile scales and their howling was tortured and forlorn. Hundreds poured forth, riding black beasts with flat tube-shaped heads, horns chipped and worn and growing at all angles, some long and some short and asymmetrical, ribs visible through their hides, and snarling mouths filled with giant human-like teeth. Their bodies of elongated limbs were naked or costumed in all manner of scraps, and trinkets, and painted symbols out of a fever-dream: severed tails; skins stretched to opaqueness; shreds of uniform still blotched with the blood of prior owners; a fine sheer blouse of pink; a necklace of yellowing teeth; a skin from a brown-furred beast; one with teeth painted all colors of the rainbow; and one with a feathered face; and one with a black leather coat that hung at the sides of his mount all the way to the ground; and one with his mount painted all in blood; and many with things woven into their hair: dangling ears and noses. And their eyes glowing fiery. And many with their faces painted all colors, grotesque and gaudy, as if death were a hilarious joke.

Already too late, the men began to scream in terror.

A foggy whistle of darts passed through the company and men slumped and dropped silently from their mounts. Horses whinnied and reared up and stomped the ground. The men gripped their weapons and watched as the horde rose up and turned full upon them with their ghastly faces and jagged harpoon spears.

The men with guns fired them and then began to reload. A second cloud of darts hissed all around. A man leaned on his knees against a fallen horse, a feathered dart protruding from one eye. Another man sat calmly in the dust, his head bent as if in prayer. A javelin made a hollow shrieking note as it lifted a man by his torso and drove him from his horse. Everywhere there were men scrambling in the dirt and horses thrashing about on the ground. One man, with frothing lips and blood leaking from his ears, was trying uselessly to pull his pitchfork out from under his horse. Another, his face a bright red, struggled with a fluted spear in his belly, as if he could still fight the invisible enemy before him. Another stared at his severed hand as it twitched in the filth and blood dripped from his arm and soaked into the surrounding maelstrom. A leathery face grinned with a mouth full of huge teeth, then flashed away in the murk.

Men tottered about, bleeding, with blank faces, uncomprehending. Tall purple-tinged silhouettes rose up and came forward upon limbs lithe like spider's legs with thin blades of black obsidian. Painted faces leered like carnival hallucinations, slicing, and hacking, and ripping limbs from still-screaming bodies; steaming handfuls of wet and glistening viscera held high and triumphantly. And everywhere there was groaning, and the babbling of prayers and obscenities alike, and men lay screaming in the dust.

"What do you think?"

The woman gasped, startled from her trance before the painting. She took a step back and looked at the artist. "I'm sorry," she shuddered. "It's quite…vivid."

"It is, isn't it?" The artist grinned, scratching his face. "Perhaps you'd care to see more?"

"There's more?"

"Oh, yes," the Artist said, still scratching at his cheek. "Much more." Scratching and scratching, until purple like a bruised fruit began to shine through and his face bled and began to peel away.

the lie

By Tara Fox Hall

Hannah Butterick was trouble. I knew it when we'd first met, in the way she looked like the twin of Sarah Palin, her makeup and hair perfect, her clothing tasteful. Why I took an instant dislike to her, I'm not sure. I just knew that it bothered me that she thought her shit didn't smell.

I didn't oppose her when she ran for church treasurer, or when she was adamant that each year she would be the one to select what cookies were baked for the women's holiday gift baskets for shut-ins. But when her desire for power grew to the point that she put her name in for election to the town board, I knew I had to put a stop to it. Hannah was not going to stop on her own. And something told me that if I didn't act now, there would be no stopping her.

I got her aside one evening after our book club let out, and told her that enough was enough. Hannah acted confused.

"I'm not sure what you mean, Irena—"

I was tired and irritated, never a good combination to inspire quick comebacks. So instead, a ready lie formed on my lips.

"I'm telling you right now, you don't stop this social climbing, and I'll tell everyone the truth," I whispered heatedly. My tone changed, becoming sly. "I know what you did, Hannah. Do you want it spread all over town? Do you think you'll still be church treasurer once everyone finds out the truth?"

She went white, her eyes livid, then walked away. Mystified at her behavior, I shrugged, and put a check mark in the win column.

* * *

"So Hannah just walked away?" my mother said curiously, when I described the scene to her the next morning. "What did she do? She had to have done something really bad—"

"I have no idea," I answered. "But at least she's not going to—" I glanced out the window, my eyes widening in shock. "You are not going to believe this, but she's here! Hannah's here! She's parked in my driveway. Some woman's with her—"

"Who?"

"Adele. You remember, the woman that's always hanging on Hannah's every word in book club—"

"What are they doing?"

I watched. "Something in the garage. I can't see. Here, take down the license."

"I don't have a pen—"

Hannah and Adele came walking out, then got back in their car. Slowly, the car began moving away down the drive.

They would get away before I had the goods to prove they'd trespassed! "Hurry and get one! They're leaving."

"Every one I try won't work—"

Fury filled me. I dropped the phone on the counter and stalked to the front door, throwing it open with a bang. "What the hell are you doing?"

The car stopped, then slowly, Adele got out, her fat body jiggling. To my horror, she pulled out the hugest revolver I'd ever seen, raising the nickel-plated gun to level the barrel at me. I slammed the door just as a bullet thudded into it, the door reverberating with the impact.

I ran for my own gun, the repeated shots deafening as they struck the door. The new sound of breaking wood and a creaking hinge sent me into full-fledged panic as I threw aside sweaters in the closet, feeling for the metal lockbox.

There it was!

I opened it, and grasped the loaded gun, standing in a smooth motion, righteous anger filling me. That bitch thought she was going to kill me. I had something for her. She'd wasted all her bullets getting in my front door.

Adele came waddling in, and I raised the gun, getting off a shot as she fired a snub .38, her gun flashing repeatedly as I fired mine. She shot into the floor a few times, then fell, the gun skittering away.

I sat on the bed, dizzy. Why couldn't I feel anything? I'd been shot only once. It couldn't be too bad. God, I had to call 911 and get help for myself.

My hands, slick with my blood, lost their grip on the gun. I fell onto my side, my thoughts rambling.

No, this can't be the end, not when I got her first, not when I'm right. It can't end this way, fading out of con-sciousness in a pool of blood...

"Adele?" a querulous voice called. "Did you get her?"

That hated voice. I grasped the gun again with effort, blinking my eyes to clear my vision.

Footsteps came slowly toward the room, hesitant and careful. Then that familiar face with perfectly styled hair and flawless makeup peeped around the corner, saw me, and froze.

"Why?" I hissed.

"You were going to expose me," Hannah said nervously, her eyes darting. "You were going to tell everyone—"

"I...know...nothing," I said forcibly, wincing at the sudden pain. "It was a lie."

Her face showed instant relief. "Then—"

I fired, the bullet striking her in the throat. Her mouth worked, trying to breathe, her hands pressed over the wound, trying in desperation to hold in the spurting blood. Swaying, Hannah fell backward, landing on Adele.

I let go of the gun, trying to breathe, then stretched out my hand towards the phone. I tried, but couldn't grasp it.

I would be okay. By now, my mom had called the police. They had to be on their way.

***

"So that's everything?" my mother said. "You're cleared on all counts?"

I nodded. "Clear self-defense. I have the two bullet wounds to prove it."

Mom smiled. "Good! We can begin your campaign."

I beamed at her. "Oh yes, right away. With Hannah out of the way, I'll have no trouble getting the nomination for town board. I'll likely even get a strong sympathy vote. Becoming the mayor is only a few steps away. And that's just the beginning."

"Just like we planned," my mom replied.

a loner in the quarter

By Jenny Bulmanski

It began in May—the slayings of loners in the French Quarter. *The Times-Picayune* and all the local news stations headline the recent atrocities. The chief of the NOPD speaks in clichés: "This department is summoning all the manpower available to protect the people of New Orleans, to find the perpetrator, and to bring this living nightmare to an end." They say it's the work of a madman with expert knife skills, and everyone should be concerned.

I should be concerned.

I walk through Audubon Park, beneath a canopy of live oaks. It's late summer, and though the sun sank an hour ago, heat remains trapped in the suffocating bubble of humidity which never leaves Southern Louisiana.

Despite the fact that some "madman" is on the loose, people are out in droves tonight. But no one ventures alone, believing the buddy system will protect them.

Once I reach St. Charles Avenue, I hop a street car. The breeze from its open windows is a small mercy.

I should stay away from the Quarter tonight—it's not safe—but I've got to get out of the house. My boyfriend has become increasingly irritating. I told him that moving in together was a bad idea—as always.

I prefer living alone. It's less complicated. When I live with someone, I try to give myself breathing room. Day-to-day conversation becomes forced and awkward, so I avoid it altogether.

He's accused me of being secretive and even implied his belief that I'm cheating on him. "Where are you going?" he asked last weekend. "It's not safe to be wandering around alone while some nut is on the loose. Or are you not going to be alone?"

Tonight I left while he was in the shower. He doesn't understand the encumbrance of living with someone. He comes from a typical family: two parents and a couple of siblings. He's accustomed to trusting the people in his home. For him, it's natural.

I, however, spent my childhood being passed around foster homes in Acadia Parish. The day I turned eighteen, I left for the city. It was frightening, but liberating. I try to live without fear, venturing alone as I please.

Trundling down St. Charles, we begin picking up troupes of vacationers at the stops scattered through the Garden District. I'm surprised there are so many, given the current state of events. But it's not as if New Orleans has ever really been safe.

In front of Slice Pizzeria, we pick up a group of what are clearly some college boys on an end-of-summer vacation. One is eyeing me and nudging a buddy. I'm obviously alone, and it's only a matter of time before I'm approached. I'm not in the mood for their solicitations, but relief comes quickly. We reach Lee Circle, and a group of sorority sisters gets on in front of Hotel Le Cirque. Their matching pink tank tops displaying some Greek emblem advertise that they're looking for a good time. The frat boys are engrossed.

Two middle-aged couples sitting in front of me begin chatting. "I'm certainly not going to go marching down any dark alleyways by myself," says one of the women, a Midwesterner. "I wouldn't anyway, but with this madman running around, who would?" She sits sideways in her seat, talking with the couple across the row, so she has a clear view of me. "You're not going around the city alone, are you, dear?"

I pretend like I didn't hear her. She repeats the question. *Nosy crone....* "Oh!" I say. "No, no. I'm meeting someone," I lie and stare out the window until my stop on Canal Street, where Carondelet turns into Bourbon. Maybe coming to the Quarter was a bad idea.

There are always police cars parked up and down the median on Canal—day or night—but tonight officers are out in full carnival force, though Mardi Gras isn't for another six months.

Bourbon Street is always packed, so you would have to be from around here to realize the crowd is acting abnormally. It's as if I live at a beach where tourists come for vacation, despite their knowledge of a recent slew of shark attacks. They still get in the water, but keep glancing down nervously. Here they walk around sipping Pat O's hurricanes, handgrenades, or daiquiris, but cautiously stay on the main path and flash obliging smiles at the officers on duty.

As the evening progresses, people begin to relax and assume the air of a typical Bourbon crowd. Merrymakers pour out of a noisy bar, music booming.

"Hey baby!" a jovial man calls and tries to dance with me. I brush him off, but he's not offended. It's late, but in the Quarter, the evening's drama is just beginning. Soon, drunks will be stumbling into alleyways, regardless of the recent atrocities and their fellow inebriates' pleas for caution.

I'm growing tired of all the noise, but I'm not ready to go home. I watch a cockroach skitter away from the neon lights into a dark alleyway. I need to get away from the light, too.

I walk down Toulouse toward the muddy Mississippi. Walking down river, I find solace in the darkness and the lull of the water. "I should go," I say to myself. *Just stay awhile,* says the voice in my head.

I've gone much farther than I intended. That's when I notice a figure hunched over in the shadows. My breath catches.

It's a man. Is it a madman? He tries to stand erect, using the brick wall for support. Just another Bourbon Street tourist, drunk and wandering alone.

He sees me. "It's you," he says, smiling, struggling to focus. It's the college boy from the streetcar.

"Hello," I say, smiling back. I approach him. It's dark here, and no one's around. I reach for the refreshingly cool handle of my switchblade.

It's just too easy to resist.

lullaby for a zombie child

By Kate Gladstone

Lullaby, sweet baby mine,
Soon we'll rise and soon we'll dine.
You will have a tender treat:
Living children's blood and meat.

Newborn cheeks and infant lips,
Toddler toes and fingertips,
Now you're of the living dead —
Close your eyes and rest your head.

Snug within my arms I fold
One who's new and barely cold.
Lullaby, sweet baby mine,
Soon we'll rise and soon we'll dine.

milk man

By Cornelius Fortune

I have a super power.

No, don't laugh. This is serious; this concerns you. You'll find this information useful.

First, let's define what a super power is: a super power makes an ordinary person extraordinary. We've come to expect such things as flight, super speed, X-ray vision and super strength as the cornerstones of superpowered ability; it's ingrained in our collective consciousness somehow.

Here's what's extraordinary about me: I can make all types of milk. Chocolate; strawberry; blueberry; buttermilk; and on my more creative days, pineapple/orange/raspberry swirl with little mint chocolate chips. I'd prefer to retain some secrets of the trade by electing not to tell you where it all comes from. It's like if everyone knew what went into the making of hot dogs and sausages they probably wouldn't eat them. Same here—you don't want to know, let's just say I have several "delivery" options.

I guess it wouldn't be much of a superpower if I couldn't make superhuman quantities of it, which I can. Call me the Milk Man if you like. I won't be offended. Honest.

Ladies and gentlemen, honored guests, UN delegates, I

don't have to remind you of the state of the world, which you know all too well.

I've struggled all my life—living on Ramen noodles, peanut butter, Kool-Aid, and I'm ashamed to say, yes, even my own milk. I've been homeless more times than I've had a permanent mailing address. But here I am before you: a super-powered being among a world of ordinary men and women.

After the plague struck I spent many a night wandering the streets, seeing headlines, watching the panic in people's faces: a world without dairy products. OMG. How scary is that? Suddenly all the dispenser buttons were switched to "off" on nursing mothers across the world; cattle died, and it wasn't because of alien invaders with a ground chuck fetish, as the extremists would have you believe. I watched the devastation, a detached observer in a world without a milkman, or any milk for that matter; we slipped into a world of imitation unlimited.

And I finally understood my purpose, at least part of it.

If you open your press kits, you'll see a list of what many of you would think of as demands, but they're not really demands—think of them more as a mutual exchange.

I'll tell you why I decided to do this now.

I've built a small army over the past year. It started as a man on the street movement, passing samples around, building friends in the neighborhood. But something strange and wonderful happened: these kids started developing mutant powers and their intelligence went off the scale. Hell, it broke the scale something awful, then they got this crazy idea about world domination, and I said as politely as I could: "Not before my morning coffee."

We started to build our PR machine, which led to you being here, listening to me.

I have a super-powered army of children with milk mustaches waiting outside these doors; we can flood the world or remake it in our image. The milk I produce alters genetic structure. I suppose old farts like yourselves could ride the wave to immortality, but what you're really here for is to provide balanced coverage of the New World Order, so I don't come off like a dairy dictator "frothing," you might say, at the mouth.

Like all movements in their infancies, we need funding. There's a collection plate going round. Feel free to place coins, dollars, valuables, and other trinkets in there. I mean, from now on, we're one big happy family.

I think when you consider the benefits, you'll see the value of full cooperation. Maybe my genetic mutation can be added as a new genetic strain for the coming generation.

And by the way, resistance is...stupid.

I'm the Milk Man, and nobody does it better than me, so let's see those pretty smiles.

There. That's better.

Children, you can come in now.

[End of Transcript]

my escape
from civilized society

By Jami Reeves

It was a dark and stormy night. Cliché, I know, but it is what it is. As it turned out, it was the right kind of night for what happened to me, but I'm getting ahead of myself.

I had just signed my biggest client to date and rewarded myself with a weekend off the grid. No computers. No cell phones. Hell, no electricity. My cousin's friend had a cabin deep in the mountains. It was the perfect place for my escape from civilized society.

Civilized, humph. How prophetic that turned out to be. But again, I get ahead.

Three side roads off the main highway led me deeper into the woods, further and further from society as I knew it. A mile down the dirt road, I came to the general store.

"Howdy, ma'am. How are you today?"

A chill ran down my back when I took a good look at my greeter. The man sat in a rocking chair on the store's porch. He looked as cliché as the night we were heading into. His stringy grey hair had not seen a comb or shampoo in sometime. I suspected that the crumbs in his long, scraggly beard were not from today's meal. He was clad in dirty overalls, his hands folded inside the bib against his shirtless chest.

Being creeped out was no reason to forget my manners. I cleared my throat and said, "Fine today. And you?"

Yellow teeth filled his smile. "Oh, I can't complain."

"Jasper! Leave the young lady alone," a voice bellowed from inside. A handsome, mountain of a man filled the doorway. Smiling and outstretching his head, he said, "You must be Martin's cousin, Serina."

"And you must be Jacob." Smiling, I shook the hand more than twice the size of my own.

"I have gathered the supplies you requested. Is there anything else you'll be needing? The cabin doesn't have a phone, but there is one here if you need it."

"Thank you, but I don't intend to make any calls."

"Well then, let's get you loaded up and on your way. You need to be to the cabin before night fall." Poking Jasper in the shoulder, he said, "Get that box off the counter and put it in Serina's trunk."

Jasper groaned and walked inside.

"My house is a quarter mile down there," Jacob said, pointing. "You'll pass it on the way up. If I'm not here, I'll be there. Come find me if you have any trouble. Are you sure you want to stay up in that old hunting shack? It's not much of a place for a woman."

"It will be great, I'm sure." I said "thank you" and set off.

Sure enough, I passed Jacob's house. Around the next bend, I saw a decrepit old woman walking along the side of the road. She smiled and waved as I drove slowly past trying not to kick up dust on her. As I entered the next curve, I glanced in my rear view mirror. The woman stumbled and fell. I jumped out of the car and rushed to her.

"What a nice girl to help an old woman."

"Let's get you up. Are you okay?"

"You are a very beautiful young woman. Such lovely skin. Tasty." The old woman licked her lips, then cackled. Actually cackled.

I felt a sharp blow to the side of my head, then nothing. I woke in a fetal position in what I could only guess was a dog kennel. I had only enough room to sit up. "I must be dreaming," I thought to myself. "This looks like something out of Hansel and Gretel." Wood walls. Wood floor. A truly dreary place.

The door burst open, and Jasper walked in. "Momma, what have you done? Why is she here?"

"Why, we're having this young lady for supper."

"Momma, we can't. Her family knows Jacob. They'll come looking for her."

"Tish-tosh. I'm going to get cleaned up. I suggest you do the same."

Jasper fell to his hands and knees in front of the kennel. "I'm sorry about this, ma'am."

Lacing my fingers through the bars, I said, "Get me out of here. Please, Jasper."

"I really am sorry." He got up and left.

As night fell, a storm descended on the mountain. Wind rocked the cabin, and rain poured in through gaps in the walls. I looked around the room, searching for some way out of my predicament. The old woman hummed while she sharpened a hatchet. When banging started in the back of the house, she grumbled, "That blasted shutter."

Jasper crept into the room when she left. Kneeling in front of me, he opened the kennel door. "You have to leave now. Quickly, quickly."

I crawled out, my body stiff from the cramped position. Jasper opened the front door. Just as I crossed the threshold, he crumpled to the floor, his mother standing over him with a bloody hatchet. She sat down and took his bludgeoned head into her lap, rocking back and forth. "Jasper, Jasper, what have you done, boy? Look what you've made me do."

I ran into the yard. With little light from the waning moon, I could barely see my hand in front of my face. I felt gravel under my feet and could make out a gap in the trees. While I made my way down the drive, I could hear the old woman wailing.

Headlights appeared around the bend. I hid behind a tree until the car was close enough to see. Jacob was behind the wheel. I flagged him down and fell into his arms. Pointing towards the cabin, I told him my story. "Jasper's dead. He saved me."

Jacob smiled down at me and said, "Well, he tried."

He wrapped his massive hands around my head. I tried to pull away, but it was too late. He'd already snapped my neck. Jacob's laughter over the rain was the last sound I heard.

need

By A.A. Garrison

It was a nightly ritual: a glass of warm milk for his daughter. Tonight, however, David poured the milk but went no further.

He was thinking.

David haunted their darkened kitchen, thinking of no one thing. The glass of milk sat over the counter, alongside a little black bottle fitted with a dropper. It was special milk, made so by the extra ingredient contained in the dropper bottle.

David was not thinking of that bottle, nor did he ever.

April. That's who he was thinking of. Not the bottle and its contents, but April, his poor, sick daughter—the center of his universe, whose gravity was irresistible. A strawberry blonde with just enough freckles, she was twenty now, though you'd never know it, the dear girl. Bedridden, grey-skinned, and haggard, April showed a misplaced age, like a new tool left out in the rain. David hated it, her illness, which no doctor could even name, much less treat.

Damn it. Damn it all.

"Damn it," David said to the empty kitchen. The milk trembled slightly.

He continued his thinking, as he'd been all night. He'd seen something on TV—that's why all the thought. It was a movie, one of those made-for-TV jobs where you don't know the actors. The plot had involved a mother who'd intentionally injured her infant child, so that it would grow up crippled and, hence, require her care.

Horrid. A horrible story about a weak, horrible woman. But David had been strangely attracted, for reasons he couldn't name.

The thinking had followed, and it was, oddly, all about April. He remembered her childhood, when she'd still been healthy and complete—a wonderful, normal child, despite being raised by a single father. Then, her adolescence: first date, first car, first speeding ticket. April had been such a whiz in school, with special classes and astounding test scores, enough to attract interest from the country's top schools. A scholarship was offered, a full scholarship, and April had been elated.

But then she'd taken sick. She'd been home ever since.

"Damn it," David said again, angered by these memories. He clenched a fist. "Damn it all to hell."

The helplessness. That was the worst, watching his dearest, most cherished possession wither away in the grip of disease—and an unknown disease, at that. They were at war with an enemy lacking so much as a name, some faceless specter free to plunder April's body at will. David had failed at protecting her, he was a bitter failure, and each day served as a reminder of this.

All he could do was give April her nightly glass of milk. Her glass of warm, special milk.

David supposed it could be worse, though. His ceaseless thinking turned in this direction: he could, after all, be alone. It was a lifelong fear of his. First he'd been orphaned, and then adopted by inattentive foster parents, who'd often condemned him to a big, lonely bedroom filled with toys for company. And then, just after his daughter's birth, he'd been abandoned by April's mother, for reasons never clarified. It had devastated him beyond recovery, and reinforced his fear no small amount.

But he still had April. Thank God for April.

Were she to leave, what ever would he do?

David blinked. He was still in the kitchen, lording over the milk and the dropper-capped bottle. April, her sickness, his razory fears—they crowded his head, refusing to leave. Also, that movie, that horrible, horrible movie. He thought of the fictional mother, crippling her child to fulfill her perverse need—horrible.

Only in fiction, David decided. No one could be so selfish.

At last, he unscrewed the dropper and squeezed precisely four drops of toxin into the milk. Doing so, he saw not the act, but only his blinding, raging need.

Upstairs, April struggled down the milk and then thanked her father. They exchanged sincere I-love-you's, and David went to bed, not alone.

the new spiders

By Elsie Schmie Knoke

"Cindy, see the gorgeous web. It must be six feet across!"

Cindy gasped, "How could she get from the tree to the car? She must have worked all night."

"I've got to get to work." Cindy took pictures as Elizabeth brushed the web away, then drove off, the ragged web trailing behind.

In the morning a web covered the passenger door and extended to the tree. Dewdrops shimmered tiny rainbows in the sunlight as it waved.

"Get it off before it eats the paint," said Elizabeth: "there's already bumps on the hood." But nothing budged the bumps.

The next three mornings found larger and more complex webs; the two women brushed off enough to open the door. The web adhered to their arms and clothes; they could barely brush it off.

Wednesday, Elizabeth awakened with a fierce itching on her arms. Her face and neck were covered with an angry red rash. Her throat was so sore she could barely whisper. She woke her roommate.

"Wake up," she croaked, "I'm sick."

Cindy rolled over. Her face was puffy, eyelids swollen, the

skin on her face tight as a drum. She lifted one bloated hand to her face and struggled to open her eyes. "Huh?"

"You look worse than I do. I think we've got poison ivy; I'm calling Joe." She shuffled back to her room and punched in his number.

When Joe arrived, he tried to hide his shock when Elizabeth answered the door.

"Something is horribly wrong. Cindy's so sick she can hardly walk." She collapsed into a chair.

Hours later, Cindy's eyes were open and the swelling had subsided. Elizabeth's rash was still angry, but the itching was under control.

By the weekend both women were back to normal. Elizabeth and Joe planned to run. Cindy hoped to take bird pictures. She gathered her equipment and went out to the car—one look and she ran back in, slamming the door.

"The car. Look at the car!"

Their little VW was completely enveloped in layers of webbing. Three spiders, the size of her hand, were busy; each was the color of coffee au lait with black spots. Their legs were translucent in the sun as they worked: one on the roof, a second swinging over the trunk, while the third worked on the passenger side.

As the women approached, the spiders paused menacingly. Joe walked over to the girls, keeping his distance from the car and said, "Hey, Cindy, call the *News-Sentinel* and tell them you've got pictures."

Cindy snapped a dozen shots of the spiders as they continued wrapping the old car in a lacy web, went into the house, and returned, cell phone in hand.

"The reporter wasn't interested until I said how big the spiders were. He thought I was joking, but asked for the pictures. I'll e-mail them. He's sending some spider expert over."

Elizabeth and Joe went running while Cindy waited.

Dr. Abele, from the University of Tennessee, arrived an hour later. A studious-looking older man, wearing a UT ball cap, jeans and tee shirt, he looked more like a student.

"My God!" he said, "I must secure a specimen. Frankly, I didn't quite believe your pictures." He pulled out a magnifying glass.

"Note the shape of this thread, like a rope: one strand wound around another. And those little projections. I wonder what their function is?"

"Careful, professor. We got a terrible rash from the web. The doctor said it was a contact poison." She shuddered.

"I wish I knew more about Tennessee spiders," he said, "The only poisonous one I've heard of is the recluse; these are much too big for that species. They must be a mutant strain. There is still nuclear waste stored around here."

He watched the busy arachnids. "I need something to keep them in."

"A shoe box? I've lots of them."

When she returned with the box, the professor moved toward the spider on the trunk.

"I'll try to get her as she swings out," he said.

He donned long rubber gloves; the spider sat quietly, watching. The two waited patiently until the man said, "I'm ready now. Bring your box up close and I'll use my butterfly net."

He finally trapped the spider. As he scooped the net into the box, the spider crawled down the handle. He tried shaking it into the box when the spider stung his right hand through the glove. Cindy brushed it off his hand with the cover, trapping it.

"You OK? Did it bite you?"

"I felt something, but I've got to get this to the lab."

Cindy stretched two thick rubber bands over the box, securing it.

He set the box down, brushing the web off his net and looked up, feeling he was being watched. Too late, he saw one of the other spiders swinging near. He stood, mesmerized.

"Look out!"

The spider landed on his neck. He brushed vainly at it. It clung tenaciously, stinging his scalp. He fell to the ground.

By the time Cindy called 911, the third spider had dropped and covered his head with webbing. His arm had turned blue, his muffled cries were weak. Cindy tried pulling the web off his nose so he could breathe, when one of the spiders stung her cheek. She tried shaking it off, but it stung her until she too collapsed, clutching the shoe box.

Elizabeth and Joe returned to find Cindy's face swollen beyond recognition and a breathing tube in her mouth. As the paramedics whisked her into the ambulance, Elizabeth jumped in and rode along.

The second team moved a body bag into the other ambulance. "Any idea what happened?" the paramedic asked.

"Giant spiders," said Joe. "Huge."

Meanwhile, hidden in the tree, the two spiders rested and planned. Both were near the end of their egg-laying cycle. Across the hills, their sisters sent telepathic congratulations. Their offspring would be larger, stronger.

night of the laughing dead

By Michael Seese

"So: Frankenstein, a werewolf, and a ghost walk into a bar. And the werewolf says, 'Am I hairy, or is it hot in here?'"

The room filled with uproarious laughter. I smiled. It did me good to hear that. It had been a while since I had played to a...um...live crowd, ever since Dirk said to me, "You'll work in this town again over my dead body." In hindsight, that was a pretty funny choice of words, considering that he's now...well, you know. I suppose there's a joke in there somewhere.

I didn't think I would want to do stand-up for the zombie crowd. No one in the business really wants to. It's a last-gasp effort to revive a dying career. But I had to face the truth: my career was on its last legs. Plus, it had been a while since I could serve up the cash to pay the rent, and my witch of a landlady was giving me the hairy eyeball.

I even had considered going on *The Late Show* out of desperation. Then, out of the blue, Dirk called and asked me to perform at his new digs. I guess the brain cells where that last conversation were stored had rotted away. At first, I said no. But then he stopped by my place—not something you want to see before you've had your coffee or after you've had your breakfast, by the way—and waved a few Benjamins under my nose.

"OK," I said, "Twist my arm." He looked at it and salivated. "That's a figure of speech," I quickly added.

I rehearsed a bunch of new material, stuff that I hoped would really kill them. I practiced, rewrote, and refined until I was blue in the face.

The big night arrived.

I wasn't sure what to expect. I feared the place would be dead. It was. And so was the clientele—not to mention, in varying states of decay. If they didn't get you, the insalubrious air of the club would.

At first, I was just falling apart up there. Absolutely stiffing. My best material was going over like hot cross buns at a vampire convention.

"What do you guys think of gas prices lately? I may go green, just to save some green. But I don't know if I can actually go out and buy a Prius. They're so slow. Usually, I get stuck behind one and find myself yelling, 'Come on! Move your Pri-ass!'"

Silence. Dead silence.

"Hey, and what about *American Idol*? Boring! I think it should be *American Idle*. You get it? Idol? Idle? Yes? No? Anything?"

More dead silence. Eerie dead silence.

And then something happened. I went off the script. I never was very good at improv, which I suppose someone who works in comedy *should* be. But I thought, *What the hell*, and just started going with the flow.

"Rough crowd, rough crowd. Literally. Seriously, have you guys looked in the mirror lately? And what's with long faces?" I said, making an exaggerated motion of dropping my jaw, and then lifting it back into place, then dropping it again, then lifting it again. "Haven't you heard of Ace wraps?"

Suddenly, I was the greatest thing this side of a gimpy sumo wrestler. Everything I said *worked*.

"You guys should see my ghoul friend. She's a sight for sore eyes. I mean that literally. You look at her, and your eyes burn."

A blonde sitting a few rows from the stage did a spit-take. Her date handed back her tongue.

"How many devils does it take to change a light bulb? One. But it takes him an eternity."

I could see that a bunch of folks had tears in their eyes. Of course, they also had tears all over their faces, and bodies.

"My buddy the mummy is thinking of going into the music business. He wants to be a folk singer. I suggested he try wrap."

Some guy in the front row busted a gut. Not figuratively.

"You guys slay me. Take my life, please..."

As they began their slow trudge toward the stage, I thought, *Bad choice of words.*

night terrors

By Alyssa Cooper

I've never been bitten by a werewolf. I've never even seen a werewolf. At least if I had been bitten by a werewolf, it would make sense.

* * *

The change was abject agony; so terrible that I couldn't scream. I woke in the night, feeling feverish and strange, and went into the bathroom. I looked at my reflection for just a moment, my cheeks flushed and my eyes all wrong, and then my head spun and suddenly I was on the floor. The light seemed to be flickering over my head, although I knew it wasn't possible, and all I could see were bleached white tiles, and the porcelain edge of the tub, and the pipes behind the toilet. It reminded me of being sixteen years old, locked in with my razorblades as I carved my imagined angst into my thighs.

My bones popped and my muscles shifted, tiny grotesque sounds in my white womb. But it didn't last long, and when I climbed up off the floor, I was standing on four legs. When I looked down at my hands they were paws, and that seemed strangely natural.

After that, I moved as if in a dream. My memories, even now, are indistinct; over-saturated and loud, moving too fast, with too many details. I had no control over my movements or of the sounds that issued from my throat. I was sure that it couldn't be real, that I was still asleep.

At first I was growling, a low hum in my throat, pacing the tight confines of the bathroom so that my claws clicked against the tiles. I whined at the door, and then like a dog, I pawed it open. I stuck my snout out first, and shouldered my way through, my tail swishing behind me.

Smells and sounds assaulted me as I moved into the darkness. A wedge of light followed me out. It lit up a narrow line of bare wall and nothing else, but the wolf didn't need her eyes. She had her nose and her ears and another set of senses that I felt, but couldn't describe and can't understand.

I could hear him sleeping—my boyfriend, in the bed. I could hear his breath and his heartbeat and his head tossing against the pillow. I could hear his blood coursing. I could smell him, overwhelmingly warm and human, and the wolf savored the scent. Her mouth started to water; it dripped from my fangs, from my shivering lips which had pulled back in an excited snarl. It dripped onto the carpet between my paws as the low sound in my throat got louder.

The wolf started to close the distance with slow, stalking steps, keeping low. She moved silently, taking me with her.

It couldn't have been the noise, but he woke all at once when I came to the edge of the bed, eyes just high enough to peer over the mattress. He sat up and looked around, blind in the darkness; but the wolf could see. Her eyes had grown sharp in the shadows. As he moved, his smell wafted towards her; his heartbeat was faster when he was awake. His confusion was sweating out through his pores.

"Cindy? Are you in the bathroom?"

The wolf growled quietly. He was afraid, and she could smell it. It excited her more than anything else had, and my lips pulled back further, twitching.

"Cindy?" His voice was shaking. "Is that you?"

My muscles tensed, just for an instant, hard as rocks; and then release. The wolf leaps, and her jaws have snapped closed before I've landed. He doesn't have time to scream, and I try to, but it echoes soundlessly inside the wolf's head. And she is not disturbed.

The first spurt of blood is hot and sudden, as the long fangs tear into his throat. He fights with amazing vigor, gurgling strangely as his hard fists come down again and again, bashing my soft nose, so that I see the pain in infuriating flashes of red. His thumb hooks my eye and the wolf whimpers without loosening her grip, and I am angry with her. I want him to hurt, I want him to see the red. The wolf resets her teeth, clawing him back when he tries to twist away, biting down on his shoulder. His throat free, he can finally scream. He tries, but it is weak. Still, it hurts my ears.

I want him to be quiet. Now.

And the wolf bit down harder, granting my request.

After that, it gets harder to remember. The wolf worked alone once he was dead, and I don't know what she did. Not really. I only saw the aftermath.

I woke up when the sun was just starting to rise, and I was in bed beside his body. I saw his face first, white skin and wide dull eyes, and that was too awful to comprehend. When I could finally stand, I realized that I was covered in his maroon blood, starting to flake away. I saw that his chest was hollowed out. And that…that was too much to bear.

I was more wild as human than I had been as wolf, tearing apart our bedroom in my rage and grief, yanking down the curtains to shred them, ripping open pillows to scatter the down and let it fall like snow. I fell to my knees in the blood and tore up the carpet pile with my fingernails. I broke apart the furniture and shattered the windows, I clawed the paint from the walls. And in the last semblance of human thought, I found a lighter in my old clothes. I lit the scraps. I set up the fire that swallowed away my life.

Now, the wolf is all that's left. She tore my life apart and she took over. I've been in the forest for years. And every heart tastes like his.

on a clear day

By Edward Lodi

The flimsy cotton jacket Bobby wore provided scant protection against the pervading damp. He shivered, brushed the residue of snow from his hair— and wished he could huddle in front of the fire that crackled cheerily in the fireplace across the room.

Pressing his nose against the glass, he stared wistfully at the outside world. Miss Rennie was in her garden, clipping the dead blossoms off her rose bushes. Old hag, bent double like some rotting stump sticking up out of the ground— so what, that he had trampled on her precious marigolds. So what, that he had called her names. Big deal!

There, limping onto the patio to sun himself and nurse his injured paw, went the primary cause of Bobby's troubles: Pumpkin, Miss Rennie's orange tabby. Mean old cat. Always chasing after birds. Always scratching around in the sand. Even now, Bobby scarcely regretted having thrown the stone.

In the street beyond the picket fence Kevin and Mark passed by on their bikes. They were heading toward the park. Bobby would have waved but his friends were not looking his way and, besides, he knew they would not be able to see him. And so the day dragged on with Bobby, nose flattened against the glass, gazing forlornly at the larger world, wishing he could go outside and play.

In the afternoon Miss Rennie took a nap, then got up to begin supper. After she had set the table, and while the greens from the garden were boiling, she went over to the window to see how her new paperweight was getting on.

Lifting it from the sill, she shook it gently, and watched as the artificial snow drifted through the imprisoned water onto the little boy's head. Poor dear, he looked so cold in that wintry scene. Miss Rennie's mouth cracked wide in a toothless grin. It was the nicest paperweight she had ever made, and was sure to amuse her for years and years to come.

on the slide

By Chuck Augello

Veronica was in the kitchen chopping garlic when she saw the little girl on the slide.

Already she was falling behind. Zach was due in twenty minutes and she hadn't even boiled the pasta yet. Their last few dates had been strained and Veronica could sense the relationship fading. She'd been picking fights, snapping at everything he said, but tonight she hoped to make amends; they'd watch a movie, share a bottle of wine, and then disappear into the bedroom.

The kitchen window overlooked the backyard, and as Veronica reached for the parsley she again saw the little girl, who was standing atop the ladder of an old-fashioned metal playground slide, the slide anchored to the lawn beneath a giant Japanese maple. The girl was young, no more than six, her hair the same blonde tint as Veronica's. She wore a pink T-shirt and white shorts, her pockets adorned with cartoon butterflies. The little girl waved at Veronica, extended her legs, and then jumped, her tiny frame propelled down the slide as she raised her arms and laughed.

Veronica gazed at the girl as if dreaming. She dropped the knife, entranced, oblivious to the pasta water until it boiled over and sizzled against the stove.

She turned and pulled the sauce pan from the burner, still not remembering that her yard didn't have a slide, didn't even have a Japanese maple.

* * *

According to Doctor Calvino there was nothing to worry about. It was just stress, fatigue, and a hyper imagination. The doctor reached for her pad and wrote a prescription for Xanax without once using the word hallucination, or the word ghost.

* * *

"Zach, I'm sorry. I didn't mean to fly off like that. I've got this presentation for the Board next week..."

"Hey, we all have bad days. Maybe you need some time...."

"What are you saying? Are you dumping me?"

"Not at all. I just think—"

"You *bastard*!"

* * *

Late for work, Veronica rushed toward the car, head down, digging for her keys in the black hole of her purse. She started the car, and almost drove away before she saw the little girl grinning in the rear view mirror.

"Do you want to hear a nursery rhyme?"

She was buckled in the back seat, eating from a bowl of strawberries, sucking the juice before biting each berry in half.

"How did you get in my car?"

"Hickory Dickory Dock..."

"Who *are* you? How did you get in my *car?*"

The little girl sang in a warm, melodic pitch.

Hickory Dickory Dock
It's time to stop your clock
This advice you should heed
Go make yourself bleed
Hickory Dickory Dock

Veronica shut her eyes, let her face drop to the steering wheel. The little girl laughed and bit into a strawberry, the corners of her mouth stained red.

* * *

"Veronica, I reviewed the data for the presentation," her manager said. "This won't cut it. The Board needs more than this. I asked Brent if he could help with the research—"

"I don't need any help. The presentation isn't done yet. I'll take care of it, okay?"

"Are you all right? You seem off lately. If there's something I can do—"

She waited for him to leave before whispering, "Go to hell."

* * *

The little girl was on the slide again, shrouded by the shade of the Japanese maple. She threw up her arms and whooshed down the slide.

"Do you want to hear a nursery rhyme?"

"I want you to leave my property."

The girl dusted her knees and ran back up the ladder, singing as she climbed to the top.

Little Miss Muffet sat on her tuffet
And took out her razor blade.

She smiled so sweetly
Then slit her wrists neatly
And that was the end of her day.

With a soft giggle the little girl flew headfirst down the slide.

* * *

Veronica rushed from house to house, banging on doors, demanding to know whose daughter was trespassing on her property. Her next door neighbor Stan was polite yet confused, but as Veronica stormed down the block and word spread, doorbells stopped being answered.

"Keep your fucking brat away from me," Veronica shouted at each door.

The police were respectful but firm when they escorted her back home.

* * *

Doctor Calvino increased the dosage and recommended time off from work. He offered to write a letter for her employer. Veronica took the prescription, but couldn't concentrate on what the doctor was saying. She didn't mention that she'd seen the little girl in the waiting room, or that the girl had been holding a knife.

* * *

An hour before her presentation Zach sent a text. *Good luck! Thinking about you!*

At her desk Veronica drank coffee and rattled her fingers against her laptop. She hadn't slept in almost forty-eight hours. The little girl had been in Veronica's bedroom all night, reciting rhymes and bouncing on the mattress. Veronica wound up curled on the floor in the bathroom, running the shower to drown out the echo of the little girl's voice.

The phone buzzed. "They're ready for you now."

The Board Room was on the fifth floor. The little girl was on the elevator, waiting.

"Please...please leave me alone."

She kissed Veronica's hand. As the elevator climbed, the little girl began to sing.

Jack and Jill swallowed some pills
And fetched a sharp new knife
With the blade at their skin
It was time to begin
And that was the end of their life.

"Please..."

"I love you," the little girl said. She handed Veronica the blade.

* * *

It was the Board Chairman's assistant who saw the blood on the floor and called for an ambulance. When Veronica's manager arrived he pulled off his jacket and covered her face. There were too many people gawking, too many people staring at the dead woman, none of whom noticed the two little girls holding hands in the corner, each softly singing in rhyme.

the pale petals of summer

By Anthony Ambrogio

Bayard Spaulding was doing dishes when he saw the three tiny figures, like characters from a *Madeline* book—pale children in paler identical dresses and hats (an almost-white pastel, like the summer flowers swaying in the breeze)—wending their way, pachyderm style (each holding onto the one in front's skirt), across the lawn in a deliberate, slow-motion procession.

A knock at the door—measured, methodical—not like a little girl's knock at all.

"Amy," he called. "Get that, please. I'm soapy."

His wife was upstairs, sitting by their feverish daughter's bedside. "What?" she cried. "I can't hear you. Someone's knocking. Can you get it?"

"I said—oh, never mind." Wiping his hands on a dish-towel, he went to answer, muttering, "A husband's work is never done."

He opened the door, flooding the shaded hallway with sunlight. The three pale little girls stood there, staring up, unblinking, through the screen door.

"Can Elizabeth come out and play?"

"What? No, sorry. She's sick. Maybe later, when she's better."

An awkward silence. The girls continued to stare. Perhaps they hadn't heard him. "Uh, I said—"

"We'll come back, then." In a single motion, the trio about-faced and marched away in single file.

Bay, about to close the door, stopped. "Wait. What are your names so I can say who—" But they were gone.

That night, a weary Amy sidled into bed with him. "How is she?" he asked.

"The same. I don't know what it is. Such a high fever—"

"We could take her to the hospital."

"Milwaukee? Fifty miles? No—"

"Why? Would it tarnish your reputation as a mother and a doctor?"

"Stop teasing."

They'd come out here so Amy could get away from big-city bureaucracy and practice real medicine. So he could be househusband and write undisturbed. But Amy was still the Caregiver; Amy still sacrificed her time and sleep and health. Elizabeth wanted Amy when she was sick. If only he could do more for them, make the sacrifices—

"*Mommy!* It hurts. I'm thirsty."

"Should I—?" he asked.

"*Mommy!*"

"She wants me."

"Better go then."

If only.

* * *

Amy dropped her medical bag on the table, inadvertently waking Bay, disheveled, dozing in a chair. Seeing him, she concealed her own distress. "Rough night?"

He shrugged. "You too, I think."

"How's Elizabeth?"

"Asleep. She drank some soup."

"I should check on her."

"Why? She's asleep."

"Bay, it's spreading. Some virus. I've seen two dozen kids this week with the same symptoms."

"Nothing antibiotics can't cure, right?"

"Antibiotics can't cure viruses!"

"Okay. Don't get mad. It's not like she's gonna die, right?"

Amy didn't answer. She went upstairs. Bay wanted to call after her, but a knock on the door—that same methodical knock—prevented him.

Same shimmering bright light blinded Bay when he opened the door. Same three pale little girls in their same pale attire, looked up at him, unblinking, serious. "Can Elizabeth come out and play?"

"She's still sick. With fever."

"That's okay."

"Do you know what fever is?" The girl nodded solemnly. "Then you know she can't come out."

"Shirley Jackson had a fever. She came out to play with us."

"Well, Elizabeth is too weak—don't play with sick girls; you might catch something."

"We'll come back."

"Okay," he said, but they made no move to leave. "Run along."

They didn't run; they slowly backed away, Midwich-cuckoo eyes still on Bay. He shut the door, shuddered. "Weird kids."

* * *

Amy paced the floor. "I'm at a loss. She's not getting better! None of them are! I feel so helpless, seeing child after child suffer—every kid in town is sick."

"Not those friends of hers—"

"Who?"

"Three little girls—"

"Their names?"

Bay shrugged. "You got me."

"I know all of Elizabeth's friends—all *two* of them—and they're both sick."

"Well, these three look perfectly healthy. Maybe a little too intense...."

"They must be the only uninfected children in the neighborhood."

"No. They said they played with Shirley Jackson—"

"Shirley Jackson *died* yesterday—I didn't want to tell you. They found her, collapsed, on her porch. I couldn't save her. What should we do? Suppose Elizabeth—"

Bay hugged Amy tightly. "She won't. The fever will break. Everything'll be okay." But he wasn't so sure.

* * *

Elizabeth lay in bed—perspiring, tossing, mumbling. Amy applied cold compresses, cooed to her, begged her to get better.

Bay, more haggard than ever, looked in on them. "Still the same?"

Amy nodded. "I'd give anything to make her well again."

"So would I. Maybe the hospital—"

"No. It's epidemic. Overflowing wards. Powerless doctors. A few lucky ones survive...."

"Let me stay with her—"

But Amy saw his condition. "Go lie down."

* * *

He awoke from a nightmare to the sounds of purposeful, precisely spaced knocking. He passed his daughter's room, saw Amy and Elizabeth both sleeping.

He opened the door, knowing whom he would find.

"Can Elizabeth come out and play?"

"No! I told you—"

"But she *has* to."

"What do you mean—'*has* to'?"

"It's time. For the game." The girl reached for the screen-door knob. Bay grabbed the handle from his side, held the door shut. "You can't stop it. She has to play with us."

"No!" Bay desperately strained to keep the door closed. It rattled from the insistent, persistent force on the other side. He was sweating from the effort. "No! *No!* Why must it be her?" He grasped at straws. "*I'll* play with you instead."

The rattling stopped. The three staring faces looked up.

* * *

Amy woke. Next to her, Elizabeth stirred, smiled. Amy felt her forehead, wept for joy, hugged Elizabeth. "Bay!" she called. "A miracle! The fever broke. She's all right!"

Amy got up, searched for him. "Bay? Where are you? *Bayard?*"

Outside, the pale flowers swayed in the summer breeze.

pyromania

By Alyssa Cooper

There is a girl walking nearly empty streets, cradled in the darkness. Her hands are deep in her pockets to save her fingertips from the cold, and her hair is hidden under a wool cap. She keeps her eyes low, on the gasoline rainbows that swim lazily in black puddles. There's no need to hurry. Nothing that could hide in the shadows can concern her.

The alleyways slipping by beside her are cloaked in inky black, starting a twinge of fear that is born in her belly and fingers its way up her spine. A heavy warmth spreads through her chest, and she smiles with teeth as she continues to walk without destination.

A moment later, she hears heavy, unsteady footsteps behind her. After letting them catch up a little, letting them creep up close, she quickens her pace. Her insides leap with the chase; the tease.

When a vice-like grip snaps shut over her arm, she is not surprised; a moment later, she is dragged away into shadows, giving all the resistance of a rag doll. She allows herself to be pulled in deep, into the rotting bowels where she cannot be seen from the street. Only then does she throw back her elbow, feeling her sharp joint connect with something soft, something with give. He groans in surprise, his spittle dripping down her neck as his grip loosens. She is free, just as she knew that she would be.

Edging back, deeper into the dark, she stares with contempt at his bloodshot eyes and greasy hair, his gapped yellow teeth as he gasps for air. Every detail of his being is sickening; she is disgusted, her teeth peeling back from her lips distastefully. Her atoms are singing, and it is only with practiced concentration that she keeps control.

The man looks down at his hands as if he expects she will still be in them. Coming up empty, he turns his eyes on her with an animalistic fury. With one hand, he draws a knife. With the other, he wipes his mouth.

"Little bitch." His voice is a snarl, his useless aggression touching her with tickling fingers.

She clenches her hands into fists, trying to hide her smile. In a smooth, easy voice, she says "I would suggest you not bring that thing near me."

He grins wide, still drooling. His eyes are cruel and hard, glittering like beetles. "I bet you would, bitch."

The warmth in her chest is growing, nearly too much to bear, and like opening a dam she allows the overflow to flood her fingers. She moans, a sound no listener could distinguish as pain or pleasure, and her eyes slip closed. A delicate heat spreads through the air around her.

She opens her eyes in time to see him charging her, running with his shoulders low and the glinting steel blade held out in front of him. All at once, she lets her power go. She lets it take over. There is a roaring in her ears and she can feel her blood pounding just below the surface. The night air burns, turning to steam, until suddenly there are brilliant orange flames leaping to life around her hands, igniting the dark. As she lifts her fists, they light up the grime-streaked walls on either side of her, her narrow face, and the staggering form of her attacker, his face dissolving into a caricature of horror even as he fights to still his steps.

The man finally stops, only feet from her, and his knife clatters to the pavement. His eyes, wide and strangely blank, reflect the orange glow as he continues to drool. The beads drip off of his chin and onto his jacket, soaking slowly into the dusty old fabric.

"What...the...fuck...."

She watches the fire in her hands with something near adoration. Tongues of flame twist around her fingers and then up her wrists, melting the synthetic fabric until it drips down to her elbows. "When I was a little girl," she says in the same calm voice, seeming to speak to the fire rather than to him, "Every one wanted to grow up and be exceptional. And I would have given anything to just be...normal."

He is staring at her, dumbfounded, when she turns her eyes back to him. She is as crazed and wild as the heat of her fire, which lifts her hair around her terribly beautiful face.

"I know better now. You," she says, pointing one flame-wrapped finger in his direction. She smiles. "You should run."

Turning sharply, he falls to the ground with his first step, his skull making a sickening sound against the pavement. Scrambling to his feet, he limps as quickly as he can, holding his bleeding head in both hands. He has not yet reached the meek light of the streets when the flames swell all around him, pressing against the walls and swallowing him, stealing away the oxygen. He freezes, smothering before he burns, opening his mouth wide to invite in air and finding only flame. The heat, so intense he barely feels it, is merciful. His end is quick, and all that is left is a blackened skeleton.

The fires die much slower, clinging to garbage cans and the man's body and their mistress's scorched clothing for as long as they can. She dampens them with a look, a touch. She sends them back to sleep inside her chest, taking them with her as she steps over the corpse and then emerges under the full moon of a street lamp.

The flames are ecstasy, a feeling she swears every time that she will never forget. But when the heat is gone and the adrenaline fades, she is left alone with a dull ache that even her city can't soothe. Like a loss, a deep loneliness, she has only the pain of passing to remind her.

the rebellious fingers

By A.J. Barry

A single severed finger falls to the floor. It's my mistake but I'm just so damn tired. I should have been using a tray to catch the fingers as I cut them from her hand. Even in this condition—recently deceased and slowly turning to mush before me—I have to admit she is almost attractive, for a corpse. But I'm getting distracted and there isn't time. We are always pushing ahead; the rush to hurry up and fail.

I notice how the fallen finger crawls across the floor—by digging its painted nail into the floorboard and then flexing like a little muscular arm. Yellow pus trails from the severed end as it drags itself a few inches under my workbench. I pick up the fallen digit but it wiggles free from my hand, like the nightcrawlers did when my pop took me fishing all those years ago. That was so long ago; before medical school; before I was married; before the dead returned to disrupt the lives of the living. Bent over, yet still seated in my chair, I search under the table and this time grab the finger with a more determined effort.

Two more severed fingers fall to the floor. They are crawling, same as the first one, but in opposite directions, trying to escape from me. Then I realize that they must still share a bond. It's a common consciousness which suggests that divided, there's a better chance for one of them to get away.

Can the fingers *see* me? They seem to sense my hand, just as I reach for them, bent over, under the table, because they curl and roll away as I try to grab the stubby, black worms. Time is wasting away. It's been a long, arduous day that has extended deep into supper time. My growling stomach reminds me that this is my last body to prepare before completing today's assignment. The three fingers are now in my grasp, under the table.

The pinky finger falls from the table, hitting me on the back of the head as it makes its way to the floor. It seems to have taken the longest to find the ledge from which to jump. Practice makes perfect and I pinch this one quickly before it has time for tricks. The growling is there again. I must be hungrier than I thought. I finally sit up in my chair, ready to tag and bag these four rebellious fingers.

The thumb is still there, resting on the table where I left it, but my pruning shears are not. She is holding them in her other hand—the one with the fingers; the one that I thought was strapped down to the table. It's another mistake. I am *really* getting tired. She is sitting up with her intestines in her lap. Her dark empty sockets are just inches from my terrified gaze.

With her hand raised above her head, she growls once more as she drives the sheers deep into my chest. I drop her other fingers to the floor, the fingers which had been distracting me, and they start crawling away again.

My screams do not alarm her or dissuade her from repeating the same stabbing motion over and over with so much of my blood splashing away from me. I fall backward, overturning the chair, and hit the floor as the security guards burst in. My sense of hearing is lost. The silent bullets they are firing obliterate the woman's skull. When they come to me, their lips carry no sound and soon their faces stretch away as my vision is drawn into a long, black tunnel. And in the momentary darkness of my mind, I wonder what will become of *my* fingers.

red squirrels

By Scott T. Hutchison

Woodrell Berger happened upon his supreme and enterprising idea when he was first having problems with a new brood of red squirrels. Woodrell was fond of feeding birds, and he'd purchased an expensive tray feeder perched on a six-foot pole—complete with a baffle—because he was of the understanding that with the tray feeder he could pull in bright red cardinals, in addition to grosbeaks, jays, tufted titmice, and mourning doves. But Woodrell was getting overrun by an infestation of red *squirrels*, who daringly leaped from the purple lilac bush—which he cut back, only to then watch them improvise, skydiving from the maples and from the roof line, landing in a scatter of black oil sunflower seeds only to set up camp while greedily stuffing their cheeks. To insure his bliss, the little things simply had to go.

Woodrell, a card-carrying metrosexual who loved women, sleek silk shirts, bright-whitened teeth, manicures, body spray, and penetrating looks at himself in the mirror, had never in that fine reflection seen himself as a killer, and so he purchased a Havahart trap to deal with the issue, baiting it with peanut butter on the assumption that he would live-capture the little intruders and their families and peacefully relocate them five miles away at the park on the other side of town.

Once the Jif was in place and the trap's lever-drop was set, Woodrell went back inside, sitting very still with a glass of merlot behind his living room picture window to take in the panoramic display of human predominance and ingenuity. Within minutes, two little chittering beasts scampered out onto his lawn, pausing every third hop and sniffing the wind. Woodrell drew in breath, anticipation suddenly beading on his scalp beneath his perfectly combed/gelled hair. His eyes widened when the smaller of the two suddenly made a hungry sprint for the trap, the larger one right behind him. The lure of food without a breakneck free fall must have been that strong—then the double mad dash of their competitive drives jolted the trigger mechanism, bringing the aluminum door down with a snap, capturing both animals inside.

The larger of the two red squirrels immediately went into a panic. He began racing back and forth in the cage, the presence of his species-mate immaterial to his need to be home, to be free. Woodrell watched him tromp over the little one innumerable times, before finally settling at one end and dolefully raging at the world.

What Woodrell then witnessed led to the big idea: the smaller squirrel, tumbled and smeared with peanut butter footprints, sat back, breathing hard, eyes wide and apparently evaluating his cellmate as the larger threat in his dire pillory of circumstance. And he was, given that circumstance, a rodent of action. As the larger captive gripped the bars bewailing the seeds of his downfall, the little guy became a red ball of feral instinct, launching himself with claws and incisors extended, going bushy-tailed postal on his sad companion's head and throat.

And Woodrell Berger, in that bloody and fur-wrenching moment, recalled the Siamese Fighting Fish of his own mean childhood, the two-bowl barrier of glass which, once the schoolboy bets were laid down, released the pent-up aggression of red fins versus blue fins with a now-in-one-bowl aquatic demonstration of the law of the jungle. Woodrell's eye had been measuring the cherry-colored Corvette on the lot of Hey-Rod's Used Cars, and he suddenly, inspirationally knew that if he could play impresario—if he could arrange caged meetings between the feisty and desperate denizens of the lost-tree world—then chittering might soon sound like chit-chinging, and he might just find himself behind the wheel and owning the world. Woodrell immediately bought eleven more Hav-A-Hearts, his own cold organ pounding at the prospects.

There have always been men who attend backwoods cockfights and dogfights, putting a week's wages on the orchestrated emotions or instincts of animals. Woodrell knew enough cock-and-bull accountants and enough "betcha five dollars" barhounds to fill his basement—which he'd renamed *Rocky's Coliseum*—and in the coming months the house took a sweet twenty percent cut of the bets, plus an admission charge, plus a fair profit on the keg beer and freshly fried-up hamburgers Woodrell cheffed on a grill in the corner for the hungry onlookers. Amidst the slavering bedlam of his customers, Woodrell listened to the sizzle of meat, attempting—and succeeding—to ignore the pressing cheers that could not drown out the tiniest of screams and death rattles.

But when the end of autumn finally arrived, Woodrell could not ignore the *scritch*ings behind his home's dry wall. The sounds—inches away from his pillowed head—tiny-footed scurries up and down, back and forth, woke him out of even the deepest Ambien-swaddled sleep. It just had to be them, in the walls, making nests for the coming cold. His success with the traps had finally fizzled, and he'd noted how the wily red devils bounded through the trees, scolding him whenever he checked on his "Humane Catch" contraptions. Tired and distracted, Woodrell Berger, rings beneath his eyes, decided to call out the big guns at Puce Pest Control.

"You got critters," the Puce-employed five-toothed scraggle of a man announced after inspection. "Could be chipmunks, could be mice, but most probably it's red squirrels. I seen 'em out there, mad-dancing. They's the toughest buggers of the bunch. Downright pugnacious. They claim territory like little kings, stand their ground, fight ya with every available tooth and nail. Gonna have to gas 'em, which means you take a night off, check into a motel, let human ingenuity and fate run their course, and then you come on back home—where you'll be king of the kingdom once again."

Woodrell picked the Maplesweet Motel located out past the north end of town because it was the cheapest depravity around. He was tired, it was late—and rounding a blind curve, Woodrell instinctively jerked the wheel hard to avoid broadsiding the deer innocently frozen in the middle of the road. His car rolled three times before coming to rest, upside down.

Hot and jagged metal pressed into Woodrell's side, searing and pinning him in. "Why me, God?" he groaned in pain, his heart beginning to race. And then Woodrell saw the bear emerge from the woods, swaggering toward the vehicle as if he had business to settle. Strangely, the deer still stood in the road, watching the spectacle with large, bright eyes. And what were those advancing from the bushes—raccoons? And bunnies? Then, from every treetop above their bestial tableau, a furry suspiration and chatter erupted in a high-pitched bark and chorus, gnawing gleefully at the dark air. Woodrell's screams raged toward heaven as the hunger in the night sounds began urgently padding and scurrying in— majestic, orderly, tooth-sharp—and everything turned red.

reflections of a family

By Bryan D. Tolin

From the passenger seat, Monica looked from the side window to her traveling companion.

"Ben...." Her voice trailed off, as if uncertain how to proceed. He answered as if she had completed her train of thought, something he was extremely good at, in an almost creepy way.

"There's no need to be nervous," he took her hand, and smiled. "They're going to love you."

She smiled back, returning the grip of his hand.

From the outside, the house appeared old. Well, okay, it actually looked ancient, but very well kept. A "stately manor" her father might have said. She wished he were here, as a matter of fact. He was an unflappable, proper English gentleman, well schooled in diplomacy and tact, old fashioned, and, in the end, a rock. He was the most stable, solid man she'd ever known. She could use his courage now, as there was something about this meeting that worried her, even though she couldn't put her finger on *what*.

"This house has been in my family for generations," Ben remarked, again seeming to read her thoughts, although her face betrayed few emotions as they drove up. She half expected Jeeves to turn up at any moment, open the car door, and lead her into the mansion. Alas, nothing so elegant occurred, and she had to open her own car door.

Ben had been unusually quiet during the trip, almost as if he were nervous as well, but didn't want to make the situation worse by expressing his concern. On only one other occasion had he dared bring a woman home to meet his family. The results were so disastrous he had since chosen the cautious, safe course of explaining the relatives away as living abroad, or not living at all—a humorous, albeit somewhat symbolic alternative.

Ben opened the front door. From the dark interior, the aroma of a thousand seasons emerged, as if a vault from an ancient tomb had suddenly been cracked opened. Inside was all the grandeur one might expect of a stately manor. Flowing velvet window dressings, what appeared to be eighteenth century paintings adorning the walls, and true 'silver' ware framed each meticulously place dinner setting. The engagement ring on Monica's finger now seemed a trifle, well, small in comparison. Until now, however, she had had no benchmark, nothing to compare, and few expectations. Ben had seemed so grounded, so humble, so...broke.

Monica nervously rubbed her hands together in anticipation of shaking, in a royal, elegant way, the hands of those in attendance. First was Ben's brother Graham. Fortunately, she had met him before, so she was spared the feeling of being thrown to the wolves, at least temporarily. Next was cousin Derek, aunt Beryl, and uncle Ken. The first were a bit nerve-wracking, but soon it became clear that uncle Ken enjoyed, to a great degree, his port. In fact, the man was plowed, and provided welcome comic relief. Too soon, it was time for the heavy hitters, those who made a difference, those to whom a good impression was important.

Ben took Monica by the elbow, and guided her into the drawing room. A fabulous full length mirror stood in the center of the room, affording Monica the opportunity to take one final glance, ensuring nothing was peeking out, and, or, no one could peek in, to private places.

All was well and in place, carry on.

"Monica, I'd like you to meet my mother Lenora. Mother, this is Monica."

Ben smiled his winning smile, while Monica extended her hand to meet Lenora's, bowing slightly. "Missus Waterford, it's a pleasure to meet you."

"We don't stand so much on ceremony here, dear. Call me Lenora." Lenora took Monica's hand every so gently. "My dear you're freezing! Warm yourself up by the fire. Ben, this poor girl needs a cup of something warm." Lenora smiled at the both of them, then glided over to Graham.

Monica was confused. Did it go well? Not so well? It was impossible to tell. His mother did show her some semblance of caring, which, in the end, meant something. She could just as easily have said, "Okay girl, off you go!" and legged it. Instead, she seemed to show genuine concern for her well-being. At least that was what Monica was going with. Ben, it seemed, was convinced as well.

"See? She loves you."

"How can you tell?" At which point Ben merely smiled and led her to the last, potentially fatal of the femmes, his sister Persia.

Persia was dressed in a long flowing black evening dress. Whereas the rest of the country—rather, world—wore black as a thinning agent to an over-exaggerated frame, Persia no doubt wore it for effect. The effect, and Persia, were both stunning.

"Monica." It was not a question, but a statement. Monica's reaction to Persia's identification was immediate. Whatever the "cup of something warm" was, it damn well better have something strong in it as well. Persia seemed to sense Monica's discomfort immediately.

"Sorry, didn't mean to frighten you. We never get to meet any of Ben's friends, so I knew you right away." The explanation seemed honest. Monica had the sense she would always know where she stood with Persia.

Ben chimed in, "Is Gran coming?"

"As far as I know," Persia replied.

Monica felt disarmed. She thought she had successfully navigated the gauntlet.

"Gran?" Ben looked at her as if he'd forgotten his keys somewhere. "Sorry, my grandmother is supposed to be here as well at some point. I'll see if mother knows when she's coming."

With a renewed sense of terror, Monica darted over to the mirror again to recheck and rethink her strategy. As she stared at her image, another reflection seemed to form in the vicinity of her eyes. It eventually grew clearer until a distinct set of two green eyes were visible, floating freely on the *other* side of the glass. Monica checked behind her, and could not locate a possible source for the reflection. She was about to call for Ben, when the eyes evolved into a black cat, which subsequently leaped through the mirror, coming to rest at Monica's feet. The cat stared up, then raised its back, and curled around Monica's legs as if wanting a pat.

Persia arrived on the scene. "Well, you've definitely won her over."

While Monica was trying to process both the cat's arrival and Persia's comment, Ben approached. "Well, I see you met Bree."

Monica, stunned, turned to Ben, who looked for all the world as if nothing extraordinary had happened. Ben looked into the mirror and continued, "Ah, here she is."

Two silvery eyes appeared in the mirror, just as they had moments before. The silver eventually turned to hazel, the eyes eventually to a face...which came through the mirror, along with the rest of her.

"Hello, my dear. So good of you to meet me. I'm Ben's Grandmother Isabell."

Monica somehow dug deep enough for a curtsey, while Ben meekly suggested, "Monica, there's something I need to tell you about my family."

Persia smiled.

saving mary collins

By A.J. Barry

The Sunday morning sun splintered through the drawn window blinds, bringing warmth and light to Robert's scruffy face. He was still holding Mary's hand from the night before. Her wedding band, which she never took off, pressed into his hand causing a slight discomfort. Like two matching pairs of a whole, their fingers intertwined creating a bond which felt like it would never be broken. Mary's hold on Robert was firm and unyielding.

How long would it be before the kids would wake in search of their breakfast and affection? These treasured moments were too few and far between. All too often it was early to rise—letting out the dog, getting the kids ready for school, and the running of errands before and after work—but Sunday mornings offered solace from that daily grind.

Robert's free hand, the one that bore his wedding band (which he also never took off), slipped down the soft stretch of skin on Mary's cool thigh. He pulled her restful leg deep between his, sliding her knee up into his groin. His arousal was quick and intense.

The chirping of birds stirred the shih-tzu still asleep at the foot of the bed. He was an old dog that enjoyed the chase in his dreams much more than those in the backyard. Two furry little legs kicked like a cyclist while he slept, in pursuit of the song being sung just outside the window.

Willing his eyelids to part and break the darkness, Robert first looked at the clock—it was just after seven—and then to the eyes of his wife. Her golden hazel eyes stared off into the distance and it reminded him of when they first met.

She was the reluctant bridesmaid at her younger sister's wedding and he was a nervous college student with more to offer from his heart than his wallet. Mary passed on the tossing of the bouquet in favor of a secluded spot on the veranda staring out into the ocean. Robert took a chance, hoping she would find her dreams realized in his eyes instead of on the distant horizon. Within a year, both of their dreams were fulfilled when they exchanged their wedding vows to become Mr. and Mrs. Collins.

Was there a sound? Patiently, Robert listened for the creaking of floorboards, the twisting of doorknobs, or a toilet flushing. Nothing. Their children were still resting.

Mary's eyes floated his way and for a moment they shared a lingering glance. Her eyes didn't have the same brilliance that they once possessed, but Robert wouldn't trade them for the world. Those precious eyes, ever-drifting in a Mason jar of formaldehyde, were the first things that Robert insisted on keeping after the accident that took Mary's life.

There was a slip in the tub one morning while Robert was at work that left Mary alone, unconscious and hemorrhaging. This led to their children's hysterical phone call after school and Robert rushing home to a find a makeshift barricade of yellow police tape. Then a coroner determined that blunt force trauma caused the accidental death which eventually delivered Mary to the Collins Funeral Home—a family business. And all of this led to the beloved corpse of Mary Collins, lying on a cold metal table and the drastic measures which had to be taken by Robert.

He knew that he couldn't go on without the ability to look into those stunning eyes, without her comforting touch, without a least one of her gorgeous legs—none of which would be missed by anyone at the wake. After all, Robert had years of experience with eye caps, prosthetics, and techniques to prepare the deceased for viewing.

Slowly, he pulled his wife's severed hand from his own, working the joints once more to ease her rigor mortis. From the closet, Robert removed a suitcase containing disinfectants and surface embalming fluids to cleanse and prepare Mary's hand and leg for storage. Taking the Mason jar from the nightstand, next to the alarm clock, he kissed each of his three keepsakes before returning them to the suitcase.

Robert cherished these Sunday mornings, knowing his time with these fleshy mementos wouldn't last forever. Saving Mary, preserving her, helped Robert cope with the loss, but he wondered who would save him from his morbid temptation to crawl down into the earth to be with all of Mary once again.

the short cut

By Matthew Wilson

Richard showed no reaction as the man shot his brother in the face.

At least that wasn't me.

Sadly, this thing was all too common. The usual penalty was a twenty-dollar fine. Richard wrapped his coat tighter around him, against the bite of the wind. The gunfire did not attract the wail of a police siren.

The dead man was not even that.

Just DNA. Data with memories.

Since the war the population had taken a natural tumble that had not flourished as expected in peacetime. In peace the living, being grateful to be alive, loved—and reproduced. But the cities were still in ruins, and depression made people feel bringing new life into such a dark world was a cruel thing.

Human numbers dwindled—until the Doppelgänger Act.

Mothers were glad their children came back from the dead, but the children were only clones: reproduced from information scraped from the shrapnel-strewn battlefield. Clones could be made over and over, as long as they had loved ones who would finance the trouble of a filled Petri dish. In time the garbagemen would come along and take the bodies away.

Their bosses would ask his mother if she wanted a replacement, while they put the trash in the furnace. Richard looked around him in the glare of the dying light.

So many living ghosts.

And not one of them was important.

I'm important, he thought with with thumping heart. He was human. Better then those copies, those poor imitations of life. When he was younger and bored of breaking windows to pass the time, he would go riding with the other humans, breaking clone skulls with baseball bats.

At least they could run faster than dogs, making it something of a challenge. The look of fear in their faces had been fantastic. But then these damn laws had come into effect protecting clones.

No longer were they property to serve and better their masters, but had the cheek to believe they were as good as humans—equals to the humans. That's why Richard liked to come to this district where the laws were not so strict and the clones had less power. Poverty kept them here in cheap houses. They had become as powerless and full of problems as any human. Just as they had wanted: equals to the humans.

After a hard day at the office, it was nice to hear the gunshots, to see the clones with holes in their faces, to rip off their smug smiles. He knew that he was quite safe. He was human. He had a card. He—

"Hey, jackass. Give me your money."

Richard turned around, offended by the smell more than by the gun in the fool' s hand. By the sway of that hand, he'd obviously been drinking. His teeth were brown when he smiled. His eyes were red when he blinked.

"Excuse me?"

—Click-clack. The man snapped back the hammer. He

was thirsty. The bars would soon close. He had problems as much as any man and wished to blot them out. "You heard, pretty boy. And your watch."

Richard sighed and produced his card from his pocket. "You cheeky—" He stopped and started again. "I'm a human. Not a copy. If you kill me you'll be hanged, not fined, idiot."

The man smiled and pulled out his own card. "Great. I'm a human, too."

The gun shot burned away the light coming down from the cracks in the distant mountain. The world turned once, and Richard hit the chewing-gum-stained floor, gasping.

"You—you can't do this." This wasn't supposed to happen to him. This happened to other people: to lesser beings.

"You bleed like a human too, pal."

"You can't—you can't do this." Richard screamed like Columbus had circled the world.

The man looked, but no one came to help. Clones walked on, minding their business. The killer was not prejudiced. Human or copy: as long as they had money, they had his time.

The gun was big, so the killer put it close to Richard's eyes and cocked back the hammer.

"So you're human. How does that make you special?"

Richard did not hear the resulting gunfire.

Or the coming garbagemen.

sleep deprivation

By Karen Tolin

Colin Corey stood in the middle of Giles meadow and gazed up at a sky awash with stars. A life-long insomniac, he often came to the meadow to relax. He looked down at six Polaroids he had taken with his new camera. He laid them out on a rock to develop, and in a few minutes he gathered them up. What he saw made the hair on the back of his neck stand on end. A moment later he was running and stumbling across the meadow toward the village and the Sheriff's office.

"You say you took these pictures out at Giles meadow?" asked Sheriff Parris, his back to Colin as he and his deputy looked them over.

Colin tried to talk, but only managed a squeak.

The Sheriff turned around and continued. "Well this one here is of the stars. So I'll agree that it was probably taken out at the meadow, but the second one...." He showed Colin the picture.

Colin swallowed hard.

"This young woman standing on a porch looking up at the stars—there ain't any homes or buildings out on the meadow, Colin." The Sheriff stared at him expectantly then picked up the rest of the pictures and thrust them toward Colin.

Colin cringed.

"Look at these." The Sheriff held each one up as he spoke. "This one shows a mob of angry people with torches. This a noose hanging from the limb of an oak tree. This is a poor young woman with her hands tied behind her back. And last but not least, in this one you have her hanging from the tree. These pictures are pretty disturbing Colin." He looked sternly at Colin. "Now me and my deputy were having a hard time believing these. We think you're playing some kind of Halloween joke."

Colin finally found his voice and began to speak quickly. "No sir, no joke. I took those pictures out at Giles meadow with my new camera. It was dark and I didn't expect them to come out. I was only experimenting." His voice cracked. "Sir, I took those pictures, but, but none of those things are there. You understand me, sir, none of those things are there."

The Sheriff looked at his deputy and winked, "What do you think Samuel?"

Samuel smiled at Colin. "What I think, sir, is that Colin here has had a bit too much to drink and is trying to scare us with a Halloween trick."

Colin threw up his hands, "No sir, I swear."

The Sheriff eyed him warily. "I'll tell you what, Colin. Why don't you let Samuel drive you home? I'll keep these pictures here in case something comes up."

Colin started to protest. The Sheriff pushed him toward the door. "Go on, Colin, go with Samuel."

* * *

After Colin and Samuel left, Sheriff Parris looked at the pictures one more time. He noticed some writing on the margins of each picture. October 31st, 1692. He smiled when he recognized himself in the angry mob, holding his torch high above his head. Then his eyes moved to the young woman standing on the porch.

"Well Sara, you almost got me this time. But I outmaneuvered you once again."

He then threw the pictures in the trash and walked out of the room.

On October 31st, 1692 Sara Giles was accused of being a witch, by one S. Parris, and hung from the oak tree next to her front porch. Her crime: She was an insomniac, and spent her nights gazing up at a sky awash with stars.

stories from the road

By Beth Lynn Clegg

Exhausted from a tough day and too many hours on the road, Tim was falling asleep at the wheel. He ignored the "No Vacancy" sign and parked by the front door. If this was like most down-home B&B's they'd have a sofa in the office, and he'd take *anything*, even slip the owner a couple of Jacksons, if necessary.

There was no sofa and the outlying cottages were occupied, but a large attic room above the office was available, provided he was open-minded and not superstitious. Number thirteen had a double bed he'd have to share with a male roommate. The man was amenable to the deal, and the reduced rate was very appealing. *Anything* hadn't envisioned this set of circumstances, but more than likely this was another bone-weary salesman counting the hours until he was home. How bad could it be? And for one night, what the hell, why not? Besides, this would be one road story his wife's bridge club would never forget.

Phil's broad smile and hail-fellow-well-met handshake put Tim at ease as he tossed his bag in the corner and collapsed in a chair.

"Long day, brother?"

"Thought it would never end," Tim said. "I'm in sales.

Seemed like every customer was impossible to please. You?"

"You might say I'm in sales," Phil said. "I'm a preacher man, trying to sell people on saving their souls by getting right with God," he said, flashing that dazzling smile. "May I assume you have a church home that keeps you right with the Lord?"

"Actually, no," Tim said, experiencing apprehension about his decision, but not about to lie. "Never felt the need. Don't get me wrong, I admire what you're doing. It's just not my thing. And talking about my thing," pulling a flask from his jacket, "I'm having Bourbon soon as I can find ice and water."

"Bathroom's on the right, closet's on the left. I'll get the ice. We can discuss this while you sip your devil's brew," he said, breaking into laughter.

"You're on," Tim said, opening the bathroom door and stepping into space, followed by screams to the quicksand below.

"Brother, choosing liquor has never pleased the Lord," Phil said, leaning over the threshold watching Tim's frantic struggle to survive.

"Help me! What kind of preacher are you? I have a wife and kids. Dear God! Please!"

"It's too late for pleading to a God, who, by your own words, 'was never needed.' You're just another sinner hoping to find last minute salvation on the pathway to hell. No use yelling. Owner's deaf as a post without hearing aids. Went to bed after buzzing me you were on the way up. Goodbye, brother" he said, shutting the door.

As the downward sinking increased, Tim brushed against something solid and held on with previously unknown strength. Willing himself to stay controlled, he inched his way up a metal pipe, struggled to free his body, dragged himself into the underbrush and collapsed.

Phil's peaceful snores greeted Tim as he entered the attic. They were quickly silenced by a blow to the head leaving him defenseless. Tim plugged Phil's mouth with a rolled sock, and tightly wound a tee-shirt around his neck. Clawing at the cloth, Phil's wild, bulging eyes relayed the terror his voice could not utter, before a final twist of cloth ended his struggle.

He pulled Phil's body to the bathroom door and kicked it into eternity, then quietly made his way back to the first floor. The elderly owner offered little resistance when startled from sleep by a noose around his neck. Draping the frail body over his shoulder, he grabbed the guest register before heading to the pit.

Tim checked his watch. He could be home in time for breakfast, but there'd be no road story for his wife's bridge club. Not this time.

swastika moon

By Joel Allegretti

Dreaming a nostalgic dream of Treblinka, *Hauptschar-führer* Ulf Englebrecht awoke in the middle of a sultry night when moonbeams bounded through his window and lit the bedroom.

He threw back the covers and lifted the mosquito net. At the window, he saw the Paraguayan landscape by turns washed in ghost and gowned in shadow. Ulf raised his fugitive eyes to the big white orb in the sky and imagined that the man in the moon had an Aryan face.

The blinds drawn, the light seeped through the spaces in the slats and drew pencil-thin line patterns on the floor. The paltry illumination afforded Ulf enough visibility to make out a dark shape by the door.

He deemed it a shadow until he saw it shift. The room's one lamp stood on a rude wooden night table on the other side of the bed. He climbed under the net, crawled across the bed, lifted that end's net, and gave the room a bath of electric brightness.

Stationed by the door was a spider the size of a coffin. Jet black and jackboot glossy, its body reflected the lamplight.

Of course, Ulf hoped he was in the throes of a different dream. The elbow he banged on the bedpost assured him he wasn't. Ulf grabbed the revolver on the nightstand. Aiming at the eight eyes, he pulled the trigger once, twice, thrice. The chambers were empty.

The spider moved toward him.

"Rafaela! Rafaela!" he screamed. The housekeeper didn't answer. "Rafaela!"

Ulf plunged under the covers and watched in icy torment as the spider climbed the net. He expected to see a red hourglass, but a yellow Star of David marked the underside of this abdomen.

His teeth chattered in the tropical heat. To comfort himself, the former squad leader sang the "*Horst-Wessel-Lied*," as he had done at rallies back home: *For the last time the call will now be blown! For the struggle we all stand ready!*

Ulf barked the party anthem's three verses again and again and again while the spider artfully took down the curtains of mosquito net and spun their replacement.

the telltale tattoo

By Karen Yochim

I'm so hung over, my hands are shaking. My palms are wet. My head feels like a machete cracked my skull. Can't get the smell of whiskey off me although I've showered twice since waking up this morning. Who could sleep with sirens, yelling, boots stomping all over the hallways of this dreary rooming house? They've cordoned off the entire building because the landlady got stabbed during the night. Millie, the old lady next door with the frizzy hair, brought me a home-baked cinnamon roll at 6:30 and explained why the police are tramping all over the place.

Detectives are going door to door, asking everybody who lives here what they saw or heard last night. I've got to get to work at Visigoth Tattoos, but they've draped neon-yellow Crime Scene tape all around the building and won't let anybody leave. And I had an appointment with my favorite client too. The little blonde airhead who wants her boyfriend's name tattooed—again—on her neck this time. I had to call in and tell the boss the cops won't let us leave.

I drank myself stupid last night down in Germaine's apartment on the ground floor. Germaine is, or was, our landlady. Once or twice a month I sneak downstairs around midnight, and we get drunk together, talk trash half the night, and sometimes have sex...if we can, after all the Seagram's we put away. And believe me, Germaine and I can really put it away!

My recollection of last night is vague, to say the least, and with this throbbing headache I have today, I can't think at all, let alone recall anything much. She slapped me for some reason. I do remember that much, but haven't a clue why. And then, when I finally staggered up the stairs to my bed, I kept hearing her nagging at me on and on in drunken dreams. She chased me in and out of my dreams—nightmares, really—her face haggard, but I don't remember what she kept nagging me about. She held me down, gouging at me with those long, crimson fingernails.

Now the detectives are stomping up the stairs to the third floor, my floor; and the racket they're raising is making my head come apart and my eyes bleed. I'm drinking coffee with three teaspoons of sugar and hot milk stirred into it, hoping I can keep it down this time. If they knock on my door as loud as they did next door, I might just throw up when I open it. Now, that would really look pathetic: a heavily tattooed middle-aged alcoholic still in his shorts and Black Sabbath tee-shirt, barefoot, and reeking of alcohol with long wet gray hair in a ponytail. Probably be a prime suspect, the way I look.

Of course, every derelict in this dump will likely be a prime suspect. Except for Millie next door who mothers all the bums, alkies and addicts living in this shithole. If an intruder did break into her apartment, and Germaine did yell for help last night, nobody living here would hear her because they all stay passed out, comatose, or in La-La Land. This building gives new meaning to the word *seedy*.

Maybe I should put on some different clothes, but wait, it's too late. The posse's already knocking at my door. They didn't spend more than five minutes interviewing Millie.

Let's hope they make it that quick over here. I've got to get to work and earn some money. I'm out of booze with not even a beer in the refrigerator...and reduced to smoking butts out of the ashtray.

I open the door and face the Long Arm of the Law. Detective Zukowski, he says. Zukowski is surprisingly tall and thin. He looks worse than I feel. Dark rings under his eyes, black hair slicked back with some stinking hair oil. Werewolf eyebrows. Where do they get these guys? He looks more like a suspect than I do. I politely let him know I have an appointment at my job.

"Okay," he goes. "This won't take long. So where were you all night?"

I tell him, "in the bed," and point to the unmade, rumpled futon over by the window.

And did I hear anything? "No. I sleep hard."

And how well do I know Germaine LaFleur, he wants to know. "I pay the rent weekly. We exchange a few words and that's it. She's polite. I'm polite. End of story."

He's scribbling all this in a spiral notebook. "And how long have you lived here?"

"Two years," I tell him.

He looks me over. "You look a little rough. Too much to drink last night?"

I put on my best sheepish look.

"You say you hardly know Germaine, right?" he asks.

I nod. When is this frigging interrogation going to be over?

"Then how come you got that?" He points to my right arm. I look down and have to grab hold of the door handle cause I must be hallucinating. There's a fresh tattoo on my forearm, mixed in between the dragon I got in '92, and the skull with a black rose I got in '95. This new tattoo is a crimson bleeding heart with a dagger stabbed through it, and

written over the heart on a wavy blue ribbon: *Germaine &*
Lenny—Love Forever—2012.

I stutter. I stammer. I gag, then throw up all over his shiny
black shoes. "I never saw that tattoo before, Detective. I
swear it!" But, Zukowski's already got a cop there
Mirandizing me, then cuffing me, and he's cursing the whole
time he's wiping off his shoes.

The worst part of this whole scenario? Last night is all
beginning to come back to me like a bloody newsflash. I start
to howl in wretched shame and agony as they perp-walk me
on down those rotting, latrine-smelling steps for the last
time.

to serve woman

By Thomas Logan

You know, some millionaires pay billions of dollars to go to outer space. Me, I got to go for free. I looked back on that big blue planet of ours, and it wasn't dumb. And in the relative weightlessness of space, I can enjoy it all guilt-free! Besides, the Rollies say they're going to carve away the pounds when we land.

The aliens, of course, they take some more getting used to. Imagine one of those two-person lumberjack saws from cartoons all rolled up over and over again into a ball with thousands of tiny mouths full of fangs that're all grabbing and rolling around, you know what I'm saying? I don't know. Okay, yeah, so they can fly through space. So what? They're like bugs with space travel. Insects. Telepathic insects. They just got an early start on us is all.

Anyhoo, the accommodations are getting a little on the smallish side, which makes me feel all kinda like I'm being kept in a cage, you know what I'm saying. I've always been real mindful of my weight. Which, I've grown out a little. I was big before when they levitated us all up from the boot camp for fatties, but now I'm like kinda really, literally "big-boned."

Really! Camp Fit's "total-life overhaul" gray sweatpants

I'd arrived in now look more like an old, gray sock lying on the floor, you know what I'm saying. Whatever. I can tell you it still beats the heck out of flying on an airplane, having to buy two seats, and those narrow little aisles no one— I mean not even crazy-skinny jogging fitness L.A. business people— can squeeze through. Just saying. Oh, and talk about in-flight entertainment! Talk about food coma! I have every channel, every show, every movie you could ever think of on demand. All I have to do to keep the Rollies happy is suck through a straw. I had no idea until just like seconds ago how all these amazing different textures and tastes all could come through a tube. I just knew it was amazing. And sucked and sucked. Mmm, and sucked some more.

Anyway, I've always been real good at sensing things and people, like how the Rollies are always kinda mentioning my weight a lot, maybe because I've always kinda been an outsider. You know, went to movies alone, ate alone. Did my own thing. Not like the dude I call Jack Sprat who freaked out yelling, "It's a cookbook! It's a cookbook!" and got dragged away by their weak little tractor beams like the crazy person he is.

Um, okay, so this one Rolly, I call him Squirrel though it could be a she, he'd always come kinda sneak in all kinda nervous, kinda a sneaky vibe, you know, being all squirrelly, if that's even possible for a roly-poly sphere that looks kinda like if a kiwi fruit mated with a metal pineapple mated with an alien from that one movie? You know the one. And maybe a ball of snakes. Anyway, the little guy'd poke and prod and take measurements with a device that looks like the inside of a geode and goes "beep-boop." And, well, the last time he came in, it tickled, and then one thing and then another and, even in so little gravity, I crushed him.

But it gets worse.

I mean "better."

So I got to worrying, which means I got hungry, and when I finally got turned around and found Squirrel smooshed and less than alive, I saw—inside—Rollies look kinda sugary like the inside of a Peep and I love, love-love-love me some Peeps. They're why Easter is my favorite holiday after Thanksgiving and Christmas, and so I just kinda dipped a finger across the top like sneaking a taste of icing. It was warm, and I sniffed the soft crystal stuff on my finger ready for it to smell like poo, but there was no odor. So then I tasted just the teensiest smidgen on the tip of my tongue, and— wow!— like a funky bleu cheese and caramel taste explosion!

That's what they'd been feeding us but weaker, some kind of one-percent Rolly milk that made me bigger, high in calories and some kind of growth hormones. And here was the full homo, the half-and-half, the breve. As the bleu cheese caramelly campfires mellowed, simmering down into a kind of heavy gouda, suddenly an underlayer exploded like picante Pop Rocks, popping and blossoming for—gosh, I don't even know—minutes? before settling into a slightly fried-batter aftertaste. Oh. My. Gosh. Heaven!

I bathed in these shapes and flavors that just danced with one another and boomed like the Fourth of July from this teensiest, little taste. Then I dipped a full finger and then two fingers in. Then tried fitting three. Then all gone. *I licked the platter clean.*

Just think, you know. I like that phrase, "just think."

Maybe I'm just a thinker.

They're like robot computers just keeping us fed; what I'm saying is they're like on autodrive. Their only real concern is about making it on time, getting us humans prepared. It's some kind of competition. For their monarchs. Like a reality show, kind of an Olympics of chef school or something. From what I gather, it's a real big to-do.

But fat chance, fellas.

Look, you can't deny what you are. I'm a big woman. And they're like a box of chocolates. They're small, strange-looking, and awfully tasty. And I'm too big to fail. My belly rumbles. All my life people have just seen the fat outside of me. But the Rollies are going to learn it's what's on the inside that counts.

Their delicious insides.

Rollies, take me to your leaders!

the tremonts have always lived here

By Colleen Shaddox

Margaret Tremont's séances encouraged the nonsense about haunting. Every time the boiler harrumphed, the Tremonts exchanged proud looks. It set one apart, having a ghost.

Ida alone was not fanciful. When Margaret awoke in torment from the assault of a malevolent spirit, Ida mentioned the three pieces of rhubarb pie her mother had eaten.

"You say that because you've never seen him. If you saw, you'd believe!" insisted Margaret.

"You've got it backwards, Mother. I don't see him *because* I don't believe."

"You're heartless!" Margaret wailed, collapsing into tears.

The Tremonts collapsed into tears frequently. They also had a penchant for bad marriages and freak accidents.

"Ghosts," they declared.

"Gin," Ida said.

Ida was the only abstinent Tremont. Margaret and Frank Tremont died in their fifties and their children followed in haste. About half were fortunate to go in accidents, while the rest made themselves sick with the drink. Their yellow-eyed ravings gave credence to the talk of haunting.

Daisy was Ida's last sibling to be taken. She died in Arizona, where she'd gone to forget a disaster of a husband. They packed Daisy in ice and put her on an eastbound train, which Ida met at 3:23 p.m., accompanied by Boone, the undertaker.

Daisy's children could not shake themselves loose from their own lives long enough to come. So Ida would do for her baby sister. She remembered teaching Daisy to crochet. The girl had the tiniest fingers.

As Ida went through Daisy's clothes in search of a laying-out dress, a chill swept the room and the house shook with demonic laughter. Ida looked for Daisy's pearl earrings. Suddenly she was lifted off the ground.

"Oh, do stop being such a pill!" Ida declared.

The laughter grew louder and darker.

"If you have something to say, then say it. I've got my hands full with a funeral."

As Ida drifted downward, she heard weeping and made out his form, something like a smudge on a sunlit window.

"Not Daisy!" he said.

"Daisy's dead. No one's left to pay you any mind."

"You've ignored me far too long, Ida Tremont. I will not be denied!"

"Mmm," said Ida, as she continued to go through Daisy's dresser.

The voice filled with spleen. "I'm not to be trifled with. In life, I killed three men."

Ida sighed. "Then why don't you go to Hell? I mean that literally."

"There is no Hell."

"That lowers my opinion of God. Well, go or stay—just don't be a nuisance."

Again the spirit laughed with bravado. "Or what? What will you, little creature of flesh and blood, do?"

"What will you do to me? Kill me with parlor tricks? If you become too exasperating, I'll leave."

"The Tremonts have always lived here."

"The Tremonts have always done any number of things that I've too much sense for. Now, where are Daisy's white gloves?"

The specter was silent, but Ida persisted. "Can't you help me find them? Never once have I witnessed you do a useful thing!"

"I'm dead," the spirit pointed out.

"Do stop making excuses," Ida said.

"I will not be treated like a servant," the spirit insisted. "I'm leaving. I'm going to go live with Rita."

"Good idea," Ida replied. "Rita's very much like her mother, our dear Daisy. She'll make a lovely hash of her life. You can take the credit."

"I'm serious," the spirit intoned.

Ida tied up Daisy's clothes in brown paper. "Mmm," she said.

As the spirit departed, there was no chill of laughter: only the sound of Ida's brisk footsteps.

under de clammy moon

By Anthony Ambrogio

Da Boss do whatever Pahouda say, cuz Pahouda get more work outta dem zombiis den any udder man. "Zombiis is easy," you says; "dey *obey*." Yeah, but dey wears *out*. Dey lose parts, doin' dat same t'ing day an' night; dey has t'be replaced. You t'ink zombiis grows on trees?—Boss gots to pay de witchdoc plenty to raise de dead. Pahouda see to it dat dem zombiis' important pieces keep workin' long after ever't'ing else be gone. Walk t'rough de plantation; you see zombiis in de fields. Come to de fact'ry; you fin' more—or less: Jus' arms, shiftin' de levers o' dem big grinders an' threshers. Jus' feet, lotsa feet, pedalin' de looms over an' over. Pahuda use 'em like a well-oiled machine.

So when Pahouda say he want Xeena, de servin' girl, Boss pay for her time, no question. Pahouda, he maybe a little rough. He love dat girl so much he love her to deat'. Papa Ton *mad*: Xeena his servant, indentured for seven year, an' now what? "No problem," say Boss. He pay witchdoc to bring Xeena back.

Now ever'body happy—'cep' Pahouda (an' maybe Xeena). He see dat girl pass by to de market or de well. She stare but don't see him with her zombii eyes. Blasphemy to want a zombii, but he want her.

Boss see how Pahouda can't do his work, mopin' 'bout Xeena. Boss say, "Blasphemy be damn! She yours!" —But Papa Ton won't sell. Boss say, "Indenture be damn! You marry Xeena, den Papa Ton lose his claim on her!"

Dat night, Pahouda and Boss, dey dig up a preacher, drag off Xeena, an', under de clammy moon, de zombii priest marry de zombii girl to Boss's foreman.

Pahouda take Xeena to de bridal shack—Boss's family cryp', done up with dead flowers—an' take up where he lef' off, figurin' Xeena endure *all* his lovin' now.

An' she do. An' more. 'Fore mornin', she wear him out but won't let go. Pahouda yell—he howl to wake de dead! Dat cry, it stir de undead in de fields, in de fact'ry. Dem zombiis drop dere tools an' join de wedding celebration. While Xeena love him, over an' over, dey rip his flesh an' tear his limbs, over an' over, 'til nothin's lef' to rend or stomp or maul—'cep' one li'l piece dat Xeena use, over an' over, like a well-oiled machine.

an unforgettable face

By Beth Lynn Clegg

Julie and her husband Ron had weighed the risks before she agreed to testify, but as the only witness to a senseless murder, she felt a moral obligation to make certain the man was put behind bars. After the guilty verdict, T.J. Crum jumped to his feet, lunging toward her. While being removed from the court room in restraints, he screamed, "I'll get you, bitch."

It had been six years since a quirk of fate put her on a collision course with a killer. Needing a loaf of bread for school lunches, she had pulled into the convenience store and was about to leave the car when the cell phone rang. Their son needed a couple of other items. As they spoke, she watched a customer wearing a hooded jacket place a few items on the counter before pointing a gun at the clerk. Arms above his head, the clerk appeared to be pleading with the gunman, but to her horror, there was a bright flash, a popping noise, and the clerk disappeared from view. Julie ducked down as the gunman scanned the parking lot before fleeing the scene. It was a face she'd never forget. She yelled at her son to hang up, and dialed 911.

Sandwich preparation often evoked memories of that grisly event. Tonight had been one of those evenings. When the phone rang, a voice from the past triggered a feeling of apprehension.

"Julie, this is Detective Calloway. I need to speak with Ron."

Apprehension turned into involuntary chills down her spine. Attempting to maintain her composure, she said, "Ron's out of town, Detective Calloway. May I help you?"

There was a brief pause before he continued. "T.J. Crum has escaped and we're concerned he'll try to make good on his threat. I don't have the particulars, but I'm on the way to get you and the kids. Grab a few things and try to reach Ron."

Suppressing a scream, she double-locked doors, closed curtains after checking window latches, and then bolted upstairs to alert the children. With a confidence she didn't feel, she assured them they'd be safe with Detective Calloway until daddy returned.

She dialed Ron's cell phone... misdialed ... damn... tried again... went to voice mail... double damn... left a message to call immediately. She threw things in a tote bag, urged the children to hurry, then went downstairs to wait. Inhale. Exhale. She felt like she was drawing the first breath in five minutes. She needed Ron. Why didn't he answer? Maybe that horrible man had been caught and they wouldn't have to leave. But what if Detective Calloway insisted they go into the witness protection program? She blocked that from her mind. That was too awful to consider.

Barely parted curtains in the darkened living room provided an undetected view of the street. Her heart skipped a beat when a police car pulled to the curb. The officer jumped out, ran toward the house, and began knocking on the door.

Julie called for the children to hurry as she made her way to the entry hall. There was another knock. "Police, ma'am. Open up."

It wasn't the detective. She pulled her hand from the knob as chills turned to icy tingling.

"I was expecting Detective Calloway."

"He's on the way, ma'am. I was closest to the house. He sent me to get you. T.J.'s still on the run."

Of course. He'd think of that. It made sense. Feeling a little foolish for keeping the officer waiting, Julie released both locks and threw open the door.

"You're lookin' real good, bitch."

vigor mortis

By Michael Spera

There are very few truly life-changing moments in a person's lifespan. Not just any event can qualify. No; a life-changing moment is something astronomical, something that shatters your preconceptions about the world, and oftentimes something very disturbing. True life-changing moments are bookmarks on the soul, and your existence is divided into two parts: before this moment and after it. One such moment for me happened one night a few years ago. It happened when I was a student in a medical school, studying for a forensics major. One night, I was alone in a lab working on a cadaver to study before a test the next morning. Was I supposed to be there alone, especially at that time of night? Not exactly, but that doesn't make the events any less true.

I had picked out an expendable cadaver and just started to make the initial incision when I noticed something flittering in the corner of my eyesight. On another examination table a few feet ahead of me, the sheet that covered the table's deceased occupant fluttered ever so slightly. Only a second or two had passed before I dismissed it as the air conditioning blowing things around and returned to my work. A few moments later, the sheet seemed to move even more. I looked up to see the sheet sliding off of the cadaver in sequence to the body actually sitting up. The sheet slid off the table entirely, leaving a nude female body looking at me from the next table over.

Now, I had seen rigor mortis before, but keep in mind that it only occurs within the first few hours of death, and rarely do the hip and back joints ever bend so stiffly that they can actually lift a corpse's torso off of the table. Even post-mortem muscle spasms are localized to wrists, forearms, and ankles. Whatever this was, it wasn't rigor mortis. I kept myself calm, put down the scalpel, and walked around to reset the cadaver. Halfway between moving from my table to the next, the cadaver casually swung its legs over the edge of its table, and simply hopped off, landing on her feet: a little shaky, but still standing on her own.

It was at that moment that I knew that I was dealing with something else entirely. I'm surprised that I wasn't terrified, that I didn't run, or that I didn't even gasp in fright. I just... stopped. The nude woman took a step towards me. She actually moved quite well for a dead person. Not gracefully, but her steps were firm, definite. She stepped with a purpose, the way a living person walks.

She came within arm's length of me and stopped. As she stared at me, I noticed how moist her eyes were, as if she were crying. The moisture reflected some of the dim light coming from above: her eyes were almost reflective for a few moments. While we examined each other, her head tilted to one side and cracked softly, as if her bones were crying out in protest against the head tilt. Her arm rose slowly and gracefully, and she ran one chill finger down my face, touching me from ear to chin. I should have been horrified. Anyone else in the world would have backed away. I can't say why I didn't. I was too curious, too stupefied. Once her finger rounded my chin, it slid off my face and her arm dropped back to her side. I'm not sure why she touched me, but it was the most human gesture anyone had given me in quite a while.

After a few more heartbeats' worth of staring, she actually spoke to me. Her voice was like a croak through her dead vocal cords, but the words were still clear. She said that she was late for an appointment. After that, she turned around and walked out of the room.

I never got around to finishing the cadaver I was working on. I tidied up, packed away my instruments, left the building, and went back to my dorm, trying to make sense of it all. I never saw her again, and apparently nobody else that was there that night saw a nude female corpse leaving the building or walking around on campus.

My perception on the meaning of what happens to the dead has changed. I now have a career as a coroner, and I've never seen another body rise, but I do spend a lot of time thinking about the one woman who did, and why she came back. Do we have a purpose that we must fulfill, even if it takes more than our lifespan? Was she a victim of some kind of karma, something that she had to atone for before moving on? Why was I the only one to see her? Was I shown this for a reason? Why doesn't this happen all the time?

Or does it?

a way yet to go

By Eryk Pruitt

The book ended no different this time than it had the pre-vious seven he'd read it. Nor did the remaining television episode. Those never do. They followed a simple, scientific formula: a daily routine interrupted and, in a pre-formated time frame, sanity must be restored.

God, if only...

Today was the day he organized all of his clothes. His closet bore shit he hadn't worn in weeks and, although the clothes had made sense when he bought them, he couldn't for the life of him explain what he had been thinking when he'd bought them, or promise he'd wear them ever again. He bagged what he could and threw the sack out back with the rest.

"Miss Haverstein isn't going to like garbage stacking up like that," he said to the empty room. "She'll be on the phone to the City again if I don't see to it." He scanned the horizon for nosy neighbors and swore he'd get to it later.

His desk was quite situated. Seven pull-away drawers tucked into coffee-stained oak, each with a clearly labeled function and papers stacked away tight and neat. If they bore files, they were alphabetized. *Mise en place*, said the French. CDs, books, magazines... everything managed down to its core. All labels in all cupboards front and faced. All recycling taken out.

He did his sit-ups, drank his smoothie, and read the article in *Fit Body* for the umpteenth time. He treated himself with a stale cookie and made note to do it again at five o'clock. He wished for a drink. He procrastinated by watching the sitcom again.

A daily routine interrupted... He closed his eyes. It had to be done. No one else would tend after it, if not him. As time passed, so did the chances to prepare for when things were set right again. The clipboard hung from a hook beneath the portrait of his grandmother. He made note that it was time to move the hook again and fill the hole born from moving the hook. Keep things lively. He retrieved the clipboard and figured now was as good a time as any.

"Howdy, Alan," he called to his neighbor. Alan Landry liked wearing shorts on his day off and, knowing Alan's wife, probably wasn't allowed to wear that particular pair anywhere but the front yard on weekends. But there stood Alan in those catastrophic shorts and t-shirt commemorating an ancient barbecue, smiling like an idiot and giving nary a shit. He made small talk, asking Alan about his wife, the weather, or the upcoming election while he recorded his notes on the clipboard, but Alan never answered. "You're not still mad about the other day," he asked Alan. Alan said nothing. He just stared up to the sky.

The neighbor across the way stood on her front porch in her bathrobe, as she always did. He waved, but she didn't wave back. Southern courtesy showed itself to the door long ago, but he took no offense. He took comfort that she probably found more interest in whatever she saw way up in the clouds. He'd get to her soon enough. These leaves wouldn't rake themselves.

Alan's lips had split. According to the notes on the clip-board, they'd dried almost immediately, then blistered three days later. He'd carried a sponge since the first week, made sure to drop water down each of their throats, but only late-ly began to wonder the point. Alan's eyes had dried and shriveled behind the sockets that held them, muscle and sinew tightened. He jotted that down and logged the date on the column next to Alan's name: *Day 19*.

Mrs. Carruthers fared no better. Once dressed for success, she had felt her dress go to tatters as she'd stopped mid-hob-ble down the sidewalk, cellphone hanging useless in her hand, face turned upward at whatever. She'd never been one to keep a secret, so he searched her face for a hint of what she'd discovered up there—wonder, terror, or something beyond belief—but she offered nothing behind eyes long ago picked clean by crows, insects, or the elements.

It went like this for blocks. David and Jenny were nice enough folk, and had now spent nearly the past three weeks in the same spot in their backyards, tending to chores. A young man had been walking his dogs. After two days, the leash had snapped and the pups had run free, never to be seen again. The young man looked only to the heavens. Old Rachel had never looked happy a day in her life, but now sat on her porch swing expressionless, head tilted oddly upward and rotting mouth agape.

All the while he recorded it, being a man bent towards sci-ence.

He squeezed the sponge into Mrs. Carruthers' mouth. Water trickled down the sides of her cheeks and onto the pavement. Nineteen days. Nineteen days without food or waste elimination or any circulation whatsoever. But he kept their mouths wet, for what it was worth. Mrs. Carruthers had been reasonably nice-looking for her age, but those days had passed. The texture of her flesh gone coarse, skin fading to a yellow hue and barely able to cover her muscles. He believed she would, if she could, ask him to let her go.

But he couldn't. Normally equipped with answers or the search thereof, he had none for why he did what he did, day after day: hauling his clipboard, pail of water, and sponge. Recording deterioration levels, notes, comments. Keeping his neighbors from going dry. Pushing the boulder up the hill. Any day now, he expected them to start moving again, for the planet to rotate once more. He fancied coming out to water them, and finding them all gone, set about finishing what they had started all that time ago before they'd stopped to stare up to the sky: laughing and thanking him for keeping them from rotting to nothing.

He looked to Mrs. Carruthers and wondered if he'd be thanked at all.

the weird zone

By Colleen Shaddox

"It's probably kids," Officer Ross said.

"If you could have heard the laughter—it was blood-curdling," Mary Jo insisted.

He smiled patiently. "You need some rest. Can anyone help you with this...?" At a loss for words, he indicated the animal entrails (Ross suspected cat) spewed all over the patio.

"I'll do it," said Sophie.

Sophie, Mary Jo, and a third actor were staying at the Barnes cottage. It sat in a row of tumbledown places where Sherman Playhouse boarded its casts. *The Weird Zone,* Ross called it. These people all had overactive imaginations. This neighborhood produced the strangest calls.

"Don't, Sophie. It's too horrible," said Mary Jo.

"Doing Strindberg in Fort Lauderdale during spring break is horrible," replied Sophie. "This is just messy. By the way, Officer, what percentage of your unsolved cases do you attribute to kids?"

"Most of them. And I'm seldom wrong," Ross said, hitching up his belt.

"Then I'm honored to be here for such a rare event," Sophie chirped.

"Are you saying you know who did this?" the cop asked.

"Not *who*. *What*. There are more things in heaven and earth than are dreamt of in your philosophy, Officer."

That's the weird zone for you, Ross thought. "If you have any more problems, Miss, just call," he said to Mary Jo and took his leave.

Mary Jo turned on Sophie as soon as the door shut behind Ross. "Really? You had to start that nonsense with the cop?"

"It's not nonsense. I've seen it before. It's method acting that does it. This becoming-the-character foolishness. Hand me that garden hose, will you? There's no question: Anya's gone over to the dark side. We may have to kill her."

The hose sent a gyrating stream of water everywhere as Mary Jo dropped it. "Are you insane?" she squealed.

"Sane and wet," Sophie said, wrestling the hose into submission. "Of course, we'd have to find another weird sister before we open. That would be tricky."

"You're talking about cold-blooded murder and your only concern is casting!"

"Don't blame me. Blame Yale School of Drama. I didn't teach the fool how to prepare for a role. It's sad really. Beginning actors should never be cast in *Macbeth*. They can't handle it."

"I admit Anya's process is extreme," said Mary Jo. "But—"

"Did I hear my name?" asked a wizened figure in a tattered robe.

"Speak of the devil," said Sophie.

Mary Jo could not believe her eyes. Two weeks ago, Anya had been a pretty redhead of twenty-three. Now, scraggly gray hair fell over her lined face. Anya smiled to reveal a mouth full of jagged teeth.

"Oh my God, is that some sort of prosthetic?" Mary Jo asked.

"Sure, why not? Watcha doing, Sophie?" Anya purred.

"Knitting a sweater."

Anya laughed, a cackle that Mary Jo found frighteningly familiar. When she opened her mouth, those sharp teeth seemed to have bits of raw meat stuck in them. "Something wrong, Mary Jo?"

"Sophie and I are worried. Frankly, honey, you look terrible."

Anya drew herself up tall. "I am terrible. More terrible than mere mortals can imagine."

Mary Jo swallowed hard. "Listen, Anya, we're concerned. Is there someone you can talk with? A doctor? A friend?"

Anya became childlike, coy. "I thought you two were my friends."

"Of course we're your friends," Mary Jo said.

"I would like to talk. There's a place in the woods where we three can meet," Anya said, putting a hand on Mary Jo's shoulder. "Come."

She shrank from Anya's gnarled fingers. "Um, I was thinking we'd take you to a doctor."

"I need only my sisters. Away with me into the woods and I will show you wonders!"

"I'd love to, Anya. But I really should stay here and help Sophie clean up. Plus we've got dress rehearsal at two. I see you're already dressed, but my make-up takes forever to put on."

"By your will or no, one day you will come into the woods with me, sister. You are mine," Anya told Mary Jo.

Mary Jo gasped. "Anya, stop this. We're not at the theater, okay?"

Sophie looked at the terror on Mary Jo's face. Her housemate was just a kid, really—young enough to be her daughter. "Ah, well, one more mess to clean up," she muttered.

"What?" asked Mary Jo.

In an instant, Sophie seemed to age twenty years. "Be still, you sputtering fool," she said. A vaguely murderous twinkle lit up her eyes as she chanted: "By the blood beneath us and the thunder above; By strangled pleading and unholy love; Let us go, sister." She extended her hand to Anya, who in turn reached for Mary Jo.

Sophie hissed. "She's not of our sisterhood. Leave her."

The pair walked away, leaving Mary Jo sitting cross-legged on the deck and crying. She could not stop, even when her weeping turned to heaving. Where could she turn for help? *Officer Ross, could you pop over and arrest my colleagues for being witches?*

After a long while, the garden gate slammed and Mary Jo felt a chill at the base of her skull. She turned to see Sophie— the Sophie she'd known for weeks, cornflower blue eyes and a ready smile.

"Let's get going, or we'll be late for rehearsal," Sophie called.

"I thought.... Where's Anya?"

"The Anya we knew was already gone. Whatever that creature was, I killed it."

"My God!" Mary Jo said, though there was considerable relief mixed with her horror.

"I'm sure he'd approve."

"But you seemed transformed, too. Just like her."

Sophie gave her housemate a wink. "My dear, that's a little trick we call acting."

"Sophie, you seem so calm. You haven't, you know, done this before, have you?"

"Heavens, no!" Sophie exclaimed, eyes wide with shock, voice tremulous.

"I can't tell if you're acting right now."

Sophie just smiled. "Let's go. Tardiness is unprofessional."

welcome to ivor beach

By Michael R. Colangelo

One day, Ben Louis walked into his office building and noted the company had seen better days. He'd been there five years—everything seemed a little worn and somehow smaller than he remembered.

He made his way down the rows to his cubicle and powered on his computer. While he waited for the machine to warm up, he checked his voice mail.

There was a message from Mary. Not the good kind of message either. A breakup sort of message.

He deleted it and skimmed his pile of morning mail. Out dropped a postcard, and it fluttered to the floor. He almost disregarded it as junk mail, but it landed writing-side up and he saw that it was penned by hand.

He picked it up and turned it over, glancing first at the picture on its face. A birds-eye view of a quaint seaside town. Stenciled above the picture were the words "Welcome to Ivor Beach." Ben had never heard of the place.

Amy, the postcard's sender, was familiar to him. He hadn't seen or spoken with Amy since college.

He read her note to him. The contents of her scrawling indicated that she missed him, that she would love to see him, and that she'd found herself in some trouble. She apologized for losing touch and for writing to him unannounced, but she had nobody else to turn to.

He put the card into the top drawer of his desk and carried on with his business for the day. At noon, he ate his bagged lunch in his car. All the while he re-read the postcard in his hand.

When work was over, he met Brad for beers at the Lion's Crown. While Ben found it lacking in atmosphere, it did indeed serve the same beers as every other drinking establishment. That was good enough for him.

Brad was one of his oldest friends. They'd roomed together in college and then stayed in touch afterwards. By some stroke of luck, both had landed jobs in the same city. They met frequently for drinks and golf.

After two beers, Ben told his old friend about the postcard.

"Fuck her. Tell her to get a Facebook account like the rest of us."

Ben continued to explain. It was, after all, some sort of beach town. Maybe the pair could use a bit of time away from the city? Maybe it was time for an old fashion road trip? The same kind of road trip they used to do back in college—like back when Ben knew Amy.

He worked through the next day and then immediately booked two weeks of vacation time. He rented a car, packed lightly, and picked Brad up on the way out of town.

They followed a handful of printout maps. Brad recited directions between drinks from a bottle of vodka that he'd brought along with him.

The directions were legion. Once they'd hit the more rural part of the countryside, many of the roads were not even marked with signs.

At some point, Ben had gotten into the spirit of things and

started taking hits off the vodka bottle too. He was only a little worried they'd grown lost. The trip seemed to take much longer than Ben thought it would.

Finally, as the sun began its descent, Ben knew that they were indeed lost. Still, they kept driving. They played it by ear based on a general idea of where the coast was. They blasted AC/DC from their car speakers the whole time. Not caring, Brad sparked a joint inside the rental and hotboxed it.

Well after nightfall, a billboard sign illuminated in their headlights. It proclaimed: "Welcome to Ivor Beach." The scene depicted in the billboard was identical to the scene displayed on Ben's postcard. He knew because he'd tucked it up in the sun visor.

They drove on. Soon they witnessed that very scene with their own eyes. Ben parked the car.

"Something's wrong."

Brad agreed.

There were no people here. No people, no birds, and no Amy. There was nothing but the scene exactly as it had appeared on the postcard.

They stepped from the car and walked towards the beach. Between the starlight and the white sands, they were provided enough dim visibility that they could see something in the water. Just offshore. It was something huge and column-like, but it swayed in the surf—moving as if it were alive.

They kept walking. Even after their shoes hit the seawater, they kept on walking.

When the water was up to their necks, Ben had to ask the question.

"What is the smallest thing in the universe?"

Brad opened his mouth to answer, but it simply flooded with seawater.

When the sea floor dropped away beneath them, wet black tendrils coiled about their bodies and continued to propel them forward towards the impossible column.

Ben knew the answer Brad would have given him anyways. It was obvious.

Us.

what he gave

By Morgen Knight

"Go, or we all die," he said. He was bleeding from cuts to his face and a wound to his side, but none of it felt serious. "Go!" he said again, and the last young hunter nodded, no more need for words. He watched the young hunters descend the elevator shaft, on steel cables, sinking into darkness. How many dead lay behind them all?

He let the elevator doors close in front of him. He was alone. He looked down the hallway and wondered how much time he had left. Twenty seconds? He could hear the creatures coming. They were called Hybrids by their own kind: a gene variant akin to certain forms of retardation. However, all the gene variant did was make them better killers. Most vampires operate with a method, he'd found. Hybrids were nearly mindless, following one or two high-functioning leaders. They formed packs, the way the Changed will, but hunted less strategically than the wolves and panthers and other creatures that the Changed became. He checked his shotgun, then fed it shells as he ran to the next door. His blood dripped on the tile. He knew that his scent was drawing them to him, stirring them into a mad frenzy that even their leaders might not be able to control. That would help. Hybrids weren't the most cautious Dark

Things he'd hunted, but in a frantic state they were easier to trick. That's how his team had pinned them on the floor below, walking them into trap after trap.

The building looked simple outside. Tall, square, brick and mortar with no windows after the second floor. It was in the old warehouse district: a one-time office building, he'd guess. But inside, the only brick walls were exterior. Everything else was new and high-tech. The building had a sterile, medical feel after the second floor; the first two gave the impression that this was an abandoned structure. That's why it had taken so long to find it.

Each floor had a different layout. He found himself blindly running through doors and down hallways. The only vampires he'd seen—beside the Hybrids—had been on the fourth floor, and he'd been with his team. The vampires had not been taken by surprise. There had been only three of them, and four of his team had died, killing two. The Hybrids had been at their rear, then, and it had almost cost them all their lives. Thank God for Cooper and his explosives, making passageways and unlocking doors in bright, impressive booms.

It was on the sixth floor—one flight below the roof–that he discovered the large rooms that had brought the hunters here.

The room was full of naked men and woman hanging from harnesses. Tubes ran from their arms, into bags that collected their blood or fed them drugs. Along the floor were gurneys with more people, all unconscious, slowly being drained. A weary moan caught in his throat. His eyes watered. He knew what was coming behind him, but he couldn't force himself to run. He walked along rows of exposed captives, their eyes closed, bags of collected blood near each, and wanted to cry. The scene made him feel hopeless. How many Dark Things had he killed? How long had he waged a personal war? Looking at them all, he knew that he'd made little difference.

Hybrids burst into the room. They were creatures with the form of humans, but they mostly scurried on all fours. Their bodies were pale and hairless. Their mouths were all razors, and their eyes were grotesquely large. He aimed at the first few, but at once they lost interest in him, leaping atop the bodies of those bound. A few woke up enough to scream as they were torn into.

It was a callused thought, but he was glad for the delay. Any innocence he'd had was lost when he'd killed his daughter, then hunted and killed his wife. He had not asked to join this war, he'd been drafted: called on to free his family from the monsters they'd become.

He ran for the far door, dropping the last package. As he ran, he shot a large-breasted woman hanging above, a black man, and a thin man, hoping it was some kind of mercy. Not enough bullets or time. They'd hoped to save them all. The best he could do was grab a young woman off a gurney and carry her to the stairwell. Up. The roof. Sunshine.

He went to the center, looked out at the city, and sat, cradling the woman as he had his daughter. They looked alike. He cradled her head.

Maybe his wounds were worse than he thought. He felt weak. The woman, removed from the drugs, stirred. Groggy. Her eyes opened, blear and clouded. He tried to smile. "We give our best," he said, waiting.

And they came. The sun did not hurt the Hybrids. They spilled onto the roof, blood-covered and enraged. The woman, sluggish still, screamed. She crawled against him. He hushed her uselessly. And from his pocket, he took the remote. It was linked to the van on the ground floor and the packages throughout. He hoped the others had gotten out.

Thank you, Cooper.

"What are those things?" she cried.

No more need for words. He closed his eyes and saw

flashes of his daughter and wife. He pressed the button. The sound was instant. The building shook, slowly crumbling. Fire erupted.

She screamed, the Hybrids leapt for the two, and as the building fell, he found that as long as he pictured his family, he couldn't feel the flames.

wolf's clothing

By John R. Mabry

A long, low howl insinuated itself into the conversation, killing it dead. The diners, frozen with sudden fear, cocked their furry heads to listen. When it came again, it was louder. Badger shuddered. "Oh, dear, dear, dear," he said, poised with his teapot hovering just over Cupcake's teacup. He swallowed hard, and adjusted his glasses with his free paw, which was shaking.

"Are you just going to stand there, or are you going to pour the tea?" asked Otter.

"S...sorry," Badger said, trying to steady himself. He lowered the teapot towards the cup, but it rattled against it, making a loud, *chinking* noise.

"Oh, dear, dear, dear," Badger repeated.

"It's okay, Badger," Cupcake said, raising one cloven hoof until he put the teapot back down on the table. "I've had enough tea. I'm jittery as it is."

"It's a wonder you didn't break that teapot," Otter said, sipping at his own cup.

The sound came again, and again it was louder—so loud that Badger could no longer hear the fire spitting in the stove. He dabbed at his brows with a handkerchief and double-checked the deadbolt on the front door. Satisfied, he sat again, fidgeting anxiously.

"I wonder what it's like to be Wolf," Cupcake said, her wool glowing gold in the firelight.

"You mean, you wonder what it's like to kill lambs?" asked Otter. "Is that what you mean?"

Cupcake stared into her teacup, her black ears twitching involuntarily. Badger felt cold despite the fire.

"Have you more sausages, Badger?" asked Otter.

Badger stared at the fire, listening.

"I say, Badger!" Otter raised his voice. "Bloody sad host," he said as an aside to Cupcake.

"Wha—oh, yes. I'm sorry, what was that?"

"Sausages, Badger," said Cupcake. "You stay there, I'll check." Pushing back from the table, Cupcake trotted into the back room towards the entrance to the cellar.

"I've never thought much of sheep," Otter commented to Badger. "But this one's got pluck."

"Oh, yes," Badger agreed. "Pluck, I should say."

Just then the house shook and a tremendous crash sounded from the back room. Badger jumped up and hugged the far wall near the front door, clutching at his chest. Otter's chair had tumbled over, and the tiny creature scampered under the table for safety. "What the blazes was that?" Otter whispered loudly.

Before Badger could answer there was a tremendous cry of an animal in pain, crashing sounds followed one after another, and it seemed to Badger that the din went on forever. Finally, however, he heard only a rhythmic thumping like the sound of meat against a board. It slowed. It stopped. Then came the sound of tearing.

"I say, Badger, open the door!" Otter was tugging at his waistcoat, the deadbolt just beyond his reach. Badger fought down his own panic, nodding, and then racing for the door.

But it wouldn't open. It had been barred from the outside, he realized, just as the sounds from the back room resumed.

They were dragging sounds. Badger and Otter clutched at each other as the wolf's head lurched into the firelight. Badger closed his eyes and waited for death. The dragging sound came nearer. The smell of blood overwhelmed him.

"I say, Badger," said Otter, jabbing at his haunch, "that wolf is limping."

"What difference is that going to make?" Badger squeaked. Strangely, even at the moment of death, he was embarrassed by the high pitch of his voice.

"Badger, open your eyes," Otter said, punching at his haunch now.

Badger blinked, and focused on the approaching doom. To his great amazement, it wasn't coming towards him. It moved to the table, and sat down in Cupcake's seat.

Badger adjusted his glasses. The wolf's head was...crooked, he noted. And his eyes were glassy, and empty of life. Blood dripped from its snout onto the saucer on the table. It was the color of soot in the yellow light of the stove. "I'll have more tea, now, please, Badger," Cupcake's voice was steady, slow, certain. Badger saw then that the wolf's head was fixed on her own, his hollowed-out brain-pan seated upon her brow like a crown. Blood continued to flow from his ear, and she pulled his skin closer about her as if to ward off a chill.

"Holy God, Cupcake, what have you done?" cried Otter, inching towards her, his eyes wide with wonder.

"It's good, I've decided," Cupcake said, the lifeless eyes of the wolf shining and dancing with the flames.

"Um....wh-wh-what's good, dear?" Badger managed.

"Being Wolf," she said, and pushed her cup towards him. "I wonder, though."

"Wonder...what Cupcake?" asked Badger, reaching for the teapot with two paws shaking almost uncontrollably.

"I wonder what it's like to be Badger."

about the contributors

Patricia Abbott is the author of over 100 stories that have appeared in print, online, and in anthologies. She is the author of a collection, *Monkey Justice* (Snubnose Press) the editor of *Discount Noir,* an anthology of stories from forty writers that all take place in Walmart; winner of a Derringer for a flash fiction story ("My Hero"), and has a second forthcoming novel in stories called *Home Invasion* (Snubnose Press). You can find more about her: http://patti-nase.blogspot.com.

Joel Allegretti is the author of four poetry collections, most recently *Europa/Nippon/New York: Poems/Not-Poems* (Poets Wear Prada, 2012). His second book, *Father Silicon* (The Poet's Press, 2006), was selected by The Kansas City Star as one of 100 Noteworthy Books of 2006. His poetry has appeared in *Smartish Pace, The New York Quarterly, PANK* and many other national journals, as well as in *The Best American Poetry* blog and journals published in Canada, the United Kingdom and India.

Chuck Augello lives in New Jersey with his wife, dog, three cats, and several unnamed birds that inhabit the back yard. His work has appeared in *Juked, Smokelong Quarterly, Hobart, Word Riot, decomP,* and other journals.

His stories will be featured in the upcoming anthologies *The Word Riot Reader* (Word Riot Press) and *Blood and Roses* (Scarlett River Press.)

Anthony Ambrogio has published film criticism in magazines such as *Video Watchdog, Midnight Marquee,* and *Monsters from the Vault.* He is the editor of and contributor to two horror-firm books, *Peter Cushing* (Midnight Marquee Press, 2004) and *You're Next! Loss of Identity in the Horror Film* (Midnight Marquee Press, 2008).

A. J. Barry is currently a high school teacher and neophyte author who dreams of writing a better horror story. He lives in New Jersey with his wife, two children and numerous furry things. The inspiration for his nightmares, visions, and interpretations come from a lifetime spent studying classic horror films, heavy metal music, and ancient cultures.

Jenny Bulmanski is a creative writing student at the University of New Orleans, located in the city responsible for inspiring this story. Initially, this story was only intended for her husband's entertainment. He enjoyed it so much she thought others might too.

Beth Lynn Clegg of Houston, Texas, is an octogenarian who began her writing career after retiring from other endeavors and has been published in a variety of genres. In addition to family, friends, and two spoiled cats, she also enjoys gardening, cooking, and believe it or not, church activities.

Michael R. Colangelo is a writer from Toronto who has published dark stories for many years in a number of venues. He is the former fiction editor of *The Harrow* (www.theharrow.com), former Member Chair of the Horror Writer's Association (www.horror.org), and presently edits an online speculative fiction zine *Ideomancer* (www.ideomancer.com). A full listing of work can be found at: michaelrcolangelo. blogspot.com.

Alyssa Cooper was born in Belleville Ontario. Her work has been featured in anthologies and magazines, and her first novel is anticipated for release in fall 2012. She is currently working as a graphic designer in Belleville, where she lives with her typewriter and her personal library.

Sara Courtney is a comedy writer living in New York. She is a freelance joke writer for *Late Show with David Letterman*, where she also works as an assistant.

Keith Deininger is an award-winning writer and poet. He is the author of numerous works of short fiction, the novella *Fevered Hills,* and the upcoming novel *The New Flesh* (June 2013). He grew up in the American Southwest and currently resides in Albuquerque, New Mexico with his wife and their three dogs. Visit www.KeithDeininger.com.

Joan Doyle, Irish artist and Spiritual Counselor, has lived in Los Angeles since 1993. She has published a collection of stories, *Spirit is Talking to You* in which you can read about her journey to a deeply satisfying life as well as the ways Spirit touches moments in the lives of twenty-six contributors for the better. You can view her art work at www.theHouseArtist.com or read about her book at www.SpiritIsTalkingToYou.com.

Cornelius Fortune is an award-winning journalist and Rhysling-nominated poet. His work has appeared in *The*

Novel & Short Story Writer's Market, Red Ochre Lit, Ray's Road Review, Citizen Brooklyn, iPhone Life Magazine, the anthology *Writings on the Wall*, and others. He is also the author of the horror collection, *Stories from Arlington*. For more information, visit www.corneliusfortune.com or follow him on Twitter @Arlingtonscribe.

A. A. Garrison is a twenty-nine-year-old man living in the mountains of North Carolina. His short fiction has appeared in dozens of zines and anthologies, and his horror novel, *The End of Jack Cruz*, is available from Montag Press. He blogs at synchroshock.blogspot.com.

Kate Gladstone makes her home in Albany, New York, where she is a professional handwriting instructor, instructional software content provider, and copy editor. Although she has been published in *ANALOG*, "Intern Shift" and "Lullaby for a Zombie Child" are her first anthologized works. She will reply by hand to any reader who correctly identifies all of the concealed wordplay in "Intern Shift."

Tara Fox Hall's writing credits include nonfiction, horror, suspense, action-adventure, erotica, and contemporary and historical paranormal romance. She is the author of the paranormal action-adventure *Lash* series and the vampire romantic suspense *Promise Me* series. Tara divides her free time unequally between writing novels and short stories, chainsawing firewood, caring for stray animals, sewing cat and dog beds for donation to animal shelters, and target practice.

Leah Hampton lives in the rural mountains of North Carolina. She teaches English and writes fiction in her spare time. Her darkest fears include worms, zombies, and the lithe, ravenous coyotes who stalk the inky woods all around her cabin.

Scott T. Hutchison's work, both fiction and poetry, has appeared in such publications as *The Georgia Review* and *The Southern Review*. New work is forthcoming in *Star*Line* and *Postscripts to Darkness 4*.

Derrick Juengst has been writing poems and short stories for about twenty years. "Arise" was inspired from a poem he wrote many years ago. Juengst has long been fascinated by horror stories and his earliest influences were Edgar Allan Poe and Stephen King.

Hal Kempka is a former Marine and Vietnam veteran. His short stories have been published in *Yellow Mama, 69 Flavors of Paranoia, Flashes in the Dark, Thrillers Killers and Chillers, Ascent Aspirations,* and *Night to Dawn* among numerous others. Anthologies include Post Mortem Press: *Shadow Play*, Pill Hill Press: *Rotting Tales*, and Blood Bound Books: *Seasons in the Abyss*. He is a FlashXer flash fiction workshop member and lives in Southern California. His email address is rvnvet6667@yahoo.com.

Morgen Knight is an award-winning horror/thriller writer whose short stories have appeared in numerous publications. She is a mother of two and enjoys vampire hunting. You can find her in Kansas City writing short stories and her first novel. Contact her at Facebook.com/writermorgenknight.

Elsie Knoke is a retired nurse/administrator, mother, grandmother and great-grandmother who has won numerous writing awards. Her stories and essays have been published in the *Chicken Soup for the Soul* books. One of her stories, "Homeless," is on CD and available from Amazon for as a Kindle download.

Debbie Lampi is a transplanted New Yorker living in southeastern Minnesota with her husband, four children, and a sheltie named Scout. She has a Master of Arts degree in Psychology from the New School for Social Research. *Shadow Play*, her debut novel, will be published in June 2013 by North Star Press.

Edward Lodi divides his writing time between fiction and nonfiction. Although he is perhaps best known for his books on King Philip's War, most notably *Ghosts from King Philip's War*, his first love is horror fiction. His short stories have appeared in numerous magazines, journals, and anthologies. Lately he has turned his attention to murder. He hasn't killed anyone—yet—but he has published two Cranberry Country Mystery novels, and is currently working on a third. He lives in a log house with his wife, Yolanda, where he is visited occasionally by a black bear who has developed an inordinate fondness for bird seed.

Thomas Logan has a variety of literary and pulp stories appearing in online and print publications and had worked in various capacities for Fictional International and smaller journals. Most recently, he's served as Fiction Editor for Issue 6 of the Portland, Ore. literary journal *The Grove Review*. Semi-reclusive and secretive, he'd prefer you not to know that he got his MFA in 2006, has lived and taught across the country, or that he often ends his sentences awkwardly.

Cynthia Lyons has been writing since she was able to hold a crayon. Cynthia lives in NY with her husband, 3 children, and a multitude of animals.

John R. Mabry is a pastor and teacher at several San Francisco Bay Area graduate schools. He is the author of many books on spirituality and religion, and also a horror novel, *The Kingdom*. He is the owner and publisher of the Apocryphile Press.

Matt McGinnis is a technical writer by day and a horror fiction writer by night. Now living in Raleigh, North Carolina on the gorgeous Falls Lake, he aims to tell stories that will compel like those of his idols, Stephen King and Clive Barker. His writing provides an outlet for his fascination with the supernatural, life after death, and the nature of good and evil.

Nick Medina is an author from Chicago, Illinois. He has been published in print, online, and audio formats by magazines, journals, and anthologies in the United States and the United Kingdom. To contact Nick, or to read more of his work, visit http://nickjmedina.wix.com/nickmedina or follow him on Twitter: @MedinaNick.

Adam Millard is the author of thirteen novels and more than a hundred short stories. His work can be found in collections from Evil Jester Press, KnightWatch Press, Angelic Knight Press, May December Publications, Sirens Call, and Bizarro Press. Adam is a member of the British Fantasy Society.

Philip Murray-Lawson runs Evolution-abc, a Paris based language consulting company. He is the author of *Heresies* (The Gothic Society), and translations of French decadent author Marcel Schwob. He has recently contributed short stories to *Vignettes & Postcards* (Shakespeare and Company) and *Emanations: Second Sight* (International Authors) both available on Amazon.

Eryk Pruitt is a screenwriter, author and filmmaker living in Durham, NC with his wife Lana and cat Busey. His short dark comedy "Foodie" has won awards at film festivals across the United States. His work has been published in *The Avalon Literary Review, Speculative Edge, Pantheon Magazine,* and *Mad Scientist's Journal.*

Jami Reeves began her writing career in 2009, although she had been writing short stories since her teen years. The native Georgian has been married for 18 years and has a son in the military. In addition to writing, she holds an Associate's Degree in Accounting and was a stay-at-home mom for many years.

Michael Seese is a former journalist, but his current day job is in information security for a regional bank. Or, as his son could say even at age three, "Daddy keeps people's money safe." He has published three books: *Haunting Valley,* a collection of fictional ghost stories centered around his home town; *Scrappy Business Contingency Planning,* which teaches corporate BCP professionals how to prepare for bad things; and *Scrappy Information Security,* which teaches us all how to keep the cyber-criminals away. Other than that, he spends his spare time rasslin' with three young'uns. Visit www.MichaelSeese.com to laugh with him or at him.

Paul Sohar ended his higher education with a BA in philosophy and took a day job in a research lab while writing in every genre, publishing seven volumes of poetry, prose, and translations. His latest poetry book is "The Wayward Orchard", the 2011 prize-winner from Wordrunner Press; his prose work "True Tales of a Fictitious Spy" was published by SynergeBooks in 2006. His magazine credits include not only *Agni, Kenyon Review, Rattle, Seneca Review,* etc. but *Horrorzine, Bewildering Stories,* etc.

Paul Stansbury is a retired city manager who lives in Danville, Kentucky. Nowadays he enjoys the time he can devote to writing. In addition to horror fiction, he has published poetry and frequently reads his work for the public.

Dede Ryan has entertained readers for decades with feature articles in national and local magazines, a novel, essays, and video scripts. She held reporting and editorial positions at *U.S. News & World Report* and *Business Publishers, Inc.,* and spent more than a decade as corporate communications director for a Fortune 500 company. Aside from reporting on Capitol Hill, this is her first horror story.

Colleen Shaddox left daily newspapers to run a soup kitchen when her editor reprimanded her for writing too many stories about poor people. While working on social justice campaigns, she's continued to write for National Public Radio, *The Washington Post*, the BBC, and many other news organizations. Her work has won awards from the National Newspaper Association, the Catholic Press Association, and the American Medical Writers Association.

Michael Spera has been a fan of horror since he was a child, collecting as many ghost stories and campfire tales as he possibly could. He has been writing horror in his spare time for at least 15 years, always trying to craft something new and to better himself as a tale spinner. Michael was born, raised, and currently lives in Massachusetts.

Diane Spodarek is a Canadian-American artist and writer who is a recipient of an NEA artist's fellowship in video-art

and two New York Foundation for the Arts artist's fellow-
ship in creative nonfiction. Excerpts from her solo show,
"The Drunk Monologues," are published in *Young Women's
Monologues from Contemporary Plays*, *The Unbearables'
Big Book of Sex*, *Even More Monologues for Women by
Women*, and *Gathering of the Tribes 2012*. She was the
"First Runner Up" at the prestigious "First Grand Poetry
Slam" at the Nuyorican Poets Café in NYC.

Gregory M. Thompson is a Science Fiction/Fantasy/
Horror writer with publishing credits in *Macabre Realms*,
Digizine, *Aphelion Webzine*, *Concisely*, *Digital Dragon
Magazine*, *Dark Gothic Resurrected*, *Midwest Literary
Review*, *Roar and Thunder*, *The Fringe Magazine* and more.
He also has an award-nominated science fiction piece in the
collection, *Steampunk Anthology*, published by Sonar4
Publications, and has a horror/western story called "Cora"
in the anthology, *Welcome to Hell: an Anthology of Western
Weirdness*, edited by Eric S. Brown. *Nightcry* and *The
Golden Door* are two of his novels, released in March and
June of 2011 respectively. For more information visit his
official site at http://www.nightcrynovel.com.

Bryan Tolin is no stranger to horror fiction. Past works
include his 2012 Tax return, his current résumé, and a slightly Photoshopped profile picture on Facebook. He hopes to
maintain these high standards in his upcoming book, *The
American Political System*, due out later this year.

Karen Tolin, originally from North Dakota, is a photog-
rapher and poet. She now lives in California with her husband and a horde of cats.

Gianni Washington is a recent graduate of the Creative Writing MFA program at Otis College of Art and Design. She loves being scared by—and scaring others with—words. She is originally from Baltimore, MD and currently lives in Charlotte, NC.

Matthew Wilson, 29, is a UK resident who has been writing since small. Recently his stories have appeared in *Beyond Centauri, Starline Poets Association* and *Carillon* magazine. He is currently editing his first novel.

Karen Yochim lives on a Bayou farm in Cajun country and writes Cajun murder mysteries. She is a lifetime horror fan of both movies and books. Her favorite horror writer is Peter Straub.